An

loving
LEAH

TRANISHA HOLLMAN

loving LEAH

inspired by love series

TATE PUBLISHING
AND **ENTERPRISES, LLC**

Published by Tate Publishing & Enterprises, LLC
127 E. Trade Center Terrace | Mustang, Oklahoma 73064 USA
1.888.361.9473 | www.tatepublishing.com

Tate Publishing is committed to excellence in the publishing industry. The company reflects the philosophy established by the founders, based on Psalm 68:11,
"The Lord gave the word and great was the company of those who published it."

Book design copyright © 2011 by Tate Publishing, LLC. All rights reserved.
Cover design by Kellie Vincent
Interior design by Christina Hicks

Published in the United States of America

ISBN: 978-1-61346-688-9
1. Fiction / Christian / Romance
2. Fiction / Romance / Contemporary
12.06.19

dedication

I dedicate this book to Bethel Baker French
(1937–2001)

Mama, I thank God for one of the most beautiful gifts
He ever gave me: you! You taught me so many things
one of them being, how to love unconditionally. You
held our family together with strength and love, and I
will never forget you, pretty lady.

acknowledgments

I want to thank God for loving me and making all of this even possible. Lord, I know it is only because of You that I have been blessed.

Thank you to my husband, Michael. Your love and support mean the world to me. I am so blessed to love you and be loved by you. I thank my three beautiful children—Nyah, Jaylen, and Jordyn—who constantly make me laugh and above everything else make me so proud to be your mother.

Doreliz Sanchez, you have always been there for me no matter what stage of life I am in. It doesn't matter if I haven't talked to you in days or weeks, I know when I need you, you are always there. Thank you for dealing with the drama. When they invented the words *best friend*, surely they had you in mind.

Shandra Small, you are my sister from another mother. You have gone on this journey with me, and you have encouraged me and supported me, and I am so grateful for that. You have gone above and beyond just being the beautiful selfless person you are and that's what makes this sisterhood priceless.

Soulesha Harden, you are my sister and friend all wrapped up into one. You helped me get through some truly hard days, and I can never repay you for that. But I want you to know that I am forever grateful. Thank you.

Yvonne Bryson, you are a beautiful person with a beautiful heart. I am so glad I met you fifteen years ago. Thank you for the friendship and all the laughter and good times. Malinda Collins, it feels like I've known you forever my friend. Thank you for always listening. It is a gift you have to listen and encourage without judgment.

Triscia Leonard, thanks for stepping out on faith and helping my dreams come true. You are loved and appreciated.

To my sisters, Courtney and Carissa Leonard. I love you both and am truly proud of the women you have become.

Max McCray, I am so proud of you, little brother, and love you dearly.

My father, Reginald Leonard, you believing in me means so much to me. The little girl in me always wants to make her daddy proud. Thank you for letting me know I have done that.

My mother, Sherran Manuel. I love you, Mom. Thank you for all you do for me and the family.

Chanika Brooks and Natasha Fabian, you are young beautiful women taking care of home, and I applaud you.

Kirsten and Dannielle Holmes, your pursuit of your dreams is an inspiration, and I want to thank you for that. Your success knows no boundaries.

Lori Ortiz, my homeslice, you have been there, and I truly appreciate this friendship. I am in awe of your strength. You are truly amazing.

Bishop Rudolph McKissick Sr. and Bishop Rudolph W. Mckissick Jr., you gave me my spiritual foundation, and it's as if every sermon was sent especially from God to you then delivered to me. In my darkest days, your words reached me and moved me forward. Thank you for being such a blessing in my life!

Jessica Stafford Knight, you have been so incredibly selfless in this entire process. Thank you so much for everything you have done. You are a blessing.

Zella Richardson and Joy Crum, when I see your faces, it's like looking at the face of God. All I can say is there is instant peace and joy whenever I have been in your presence.

Patricia Hodge, thank you for your genius ideas and knowledge. They are appreciated.

Carol Small, B.K.A. Aunt Carol, what can I say. Almost from birth you encouraged me and told me I could do anything I put my mind to. Thank you so much for all the love and support throughout my entire life. I love you!

Michael Small Jr., more like my brother than my cousin, you have been a strong positive force in my life. I can't put into words how you have been there for me and Nyah. Love you, brother.

Julie Tookes, thank you for being who you are and caring the way you do.

Ryan Plaza, You are an inspiration to your generation as well as mine. Your success is limitless!

Sonya Valcin, thank you for so many great childhood memories. We have smiled and laughed together so many times over the years. I love you, my friend.

Christy Lloyd, no matter how much time passes, you are always there, friend, no matter what. Thank you for everything.

Mario Small, Marquis Small, and Makeevan Small, all three of you keep me laughing. I love you, family.

My mother-in-law, Ilene Hollman, you are such a giver. I love you and thank you. Cassandra Hollman, thank you for using the powerful gift of prayer that God gave you.

Shakisha Edness, my sister in Christ. The world will know your voice and words as little drops of joy for the soul. You are a gift from God! I also want to thank you for the prayer line that changed my life.

Ms. Barbara, thank you for your prayers and words of wisdom.

Vanessa Hollman, keep dreaming your dreams. They will come true!

Ketoura Battle, my little big sister. You are wise beyond your years, my friend.

Africa Lewis, you have made me laugh until I cry, and there have been so many times when I have needed that. Thank you.

Rosemary and Wyman Winbush, God's loving light shines on you both, and it just brings happiness and joy to all those around you.

My proofreaders: Lori, Ketoura, and Rose, thank you for your incredible insight.

Bertha Leonard,Grandma,you have always had the sweetest spirit. I love you and thank you for being the sweet and kind person you are. Melissa Summerville, I truly appreciate all of your support and encouragement, thank you!

Chloe Cahill, thank you for using your talent to help and encourage.

Sandra Simon, you are such an awesome, mighty woman of God. His love and peace shine on you. Thank you for being a blessing and letting your light shine.

Violet Houston, Virginia Perry, Gary Manuel, Emma-Jo Johnson, Kayatana Holmes, Tameca Wade: your entire family just gives in a way that is so selfless it takes my breath away and humbles me. Thank you!

My editor, Ashley Luckett, you are phenomenal!

Shawna Green and Maria Green, I have had some of the best times of my life with you and your family. Thank you for the great memories, great food and we can't forget that lemonade...

To all my friends and family, I love you and thank you!

God Sends Angels Every Day.

I am a firm believer that God sends angels to us every day. In my life, this has happened to me many times, and I am so thankful to Jesus Christ for these blessings. Whether it's been a family member, friend, someone from church, or even a complete stranger, God has truly shown me how blessed and loved I am when he puts these specific people in my path at a specific time.

Chris Courtenay

I remember one night after Bible study I was on my way to my car and I ran into you. You asked how I was and how the family was, and I gave you that initial surface answer. But you saw through that, and out of concern, you asked what was wrong. Like a dam breaking, words rushed forth as I began to talk. I know I had to go on for at least an hour, and you never interrupted, never looked at your watch, never stopped me with an impatient look. After that hour, I just felt a peace. You never judged, and you encouraged me. Thank you, man of God, for letting God use you!

Patrice McConnell

One Sunday, I fought my way to church. It was one of those Sundays where the enemy had thrown everything at me to keep me from going to church. Feelings of worry, fear, stress, insecurities, and anger grabbed hold of me and refused to let go. I felt depressed and just down and out that morning, but I knew I had to get there. When I got to church, you were the first person I saw, and as soon as you saw me, you hugged me and smiled. That smile was as bright as the sun, and then you told me how pretty I looked. I was like, *Is she seeing* me? because I didn't see that when I looked in the mirror that morning. I looked at your face, and you genuinely meant it, and in that instant my spirits lifted and gone were the clouds of depression. Your positive words and smile snatched me right out of the darkness, and I will forever be grateful for that day.

Woman at the store

Last week I went to the store to pick up a few things. When I got to the cash register, the woman in front of me turned around and spoke and asked me how I was doing. I said "Fine" and smiled at her. She then turned to the cash register and said to the cashier, "I am going to pay for her things too." I was shocked; she was a complete stranger. I was like, "Ma'am, are you sure?" She said, "Yes, today is your day." She paid for her things and mine, and I thanked God because that blessing could only come from Him. I don't know her name, but God does, and He will bless her life in a major way!

chapter 1

Staring out the window, I could see the sun shining. It was a beautiful day, but still no Bryce. I glanced at my watch nervously. It was now 5:55 p.m.; he was fifty-five minutes late. He hadn't even called me to let me know what was going on. Reaching for my cell phone, I tried to call him again, but still no answer. I threw my phone down on the bed in frustration. As I checked my appearance in the mirror, I let my mind take me back to a place and time when Bryce Gordon wouldn't have made me wait for anything, a time when I never even questioned my importance to him.

It all seemed so long ago. I'd met Bryce during college, and when we'd first started dating, I really didn't think it would be anything serious. I had experienced enough heartache with my son's father. I couldn't honestly see myself letting anyone else in again like that. And I was focused on making a good life for Darren and me. So in the beginning, Bryce was just someone I would hang out with from time to time. But as time went on, he really grew on me. It was as if he couldn't spend enough time with me. His persistence just blew me away and he seemed to always want to be near me.

We used to talk forever about any and everything. We would take long walks on the beach or just jump in the car and ride anywhere the wind would take us. Before I knew it, I had fallen in love with Bryce; it seemed like such a lifetime ago.

The sound of my cell phone ringing snapped me out my thoughts of the past. "Hello," I said hurriedly, hoping this was Bryce.

"Leah, I'm not going to make it tonight. We have a new client, and something has just come up." Bryce was the owner of five real estate companies in the state of Georgia, and something was always "coming up." Inside I was screaming.

"Bryce, this is our ten-year anniversary. I have been planning this for weeks," I said, panicking. I thought of all the preparation I'd put into this night. First, we would have dinner at Anthony's. It was one of the most exclusive, romantic restaurants in the city, and you had to make reservations weeks in advance.

After dinner, I'd planned for us to attend the new award-winning romantic play, *Yo Todavia Estoy Enamorada De Ti*, which means I'm still in love with you. I had really lucked out on that one, because the play was only in Atlanta for one night and it had been sold out, but at the last minute, a friend of mine had called asking if I could use her tickets. When I looked at the date, I couldn't believe my good luck.

And then for the grand finale, we were to end up at the Hilton Garden of Atlanta, where we would spend the entire evening reminding each other over and over again of how the fire between us began. We needed this night; this was our night. "Well, Leah, there's nothing I can do about this, it's important. You'll have to plan this little dinner some other night," Bryce said impatiently.

"What about our anniversary? Isn't that important to you?" I could hear my voice getting out of control, but I couldn't help myself.

"Here you go with the drama," he said sarcastically.

"Bryce, I understand your job is important, but, baby, tonight is special. It's just you and me, celebrating ten years. Nothing should be more important than that.

"Leah," he yelled my name as if it were an accusation. "This is business, and I don't have time for your drama. I have to go. I'll be home late, so don't wait up. And by the way, happy anniversary." He ended the conversation by just hanging up. Feeling stunned, I stood there frozen for a moment.

Sick and disgusted, I sat down on the bed. I couldn't believe he was doing this to me. Who was this stranger that had taken over my husband's body? Tears began streaming down my face as the hurt and pain stabbed at my heart. It wasn't just about tonight. Our marriage had been going downhill for the last five years, and the distance between us was just continuing to grow. I turned and faced the mirror. In that moment I didn't recognize myself anymore. My newly done micro braids were swept up into a sophisticated yet sexy updo. The diamond stud earrings sparkled, and I touched them for a moment, remembering that they'd been my fifth-year anniversary present from Bryce. I remembered how excited and happy I'd been. Standing up, I struggled to keep my emotions in check. I smoothed my hands over my dress in an effort to keep myself busy. My dress, an original Vera Wang, hugged my curves in all the right places. I'd found the perfect shoes and baby blue evening bag to match. It was the eyes that told a different story. I'd always received compliments about my deep brown eyes that were slightly slanted, giving me an almost exotic look. But if you really looked into these eyes, you could see a deep, swirling pool of sadness. As I stared at myself in the mirror, my knees began to shake. Feeling weak, I sat down on the bed just as the phone rang.

Planning to ignore the phone, I got up to turn the ringer off. I wasn't in the mood to talk to anyone right now. I'd have to pretend. And I didn't have the energy to pretend that everything was okay, to pretend that my heart wasn't aching. Pretending was all I seem to do lately. Glancing at the caller ID, I recognized the number right away. It was my grandmother Clara-Ann Brinkley. Immediately the knot in my stomach began to loosen and the pain began to lessen. If there was one person I could be real with, one person who truly knew me, it was my grandma. "Hello, Granny," I said answering the phone.

"How's my girl?" she asked. No matter how old I got; hearing her say that always put a smile on my face and made me think of fond childhood memories. It had always just been my mother, Granny and me since my father had left the scene as soon as he found out my mother was pregnant with me. Granny and I had always had a real close relationship. I was truly happy to hear from her tonight, I just didn't want to discuss everything right now. "Your girl is fine Granny."

"So have you prayed about it?" she asked me.

"Prayed about what?" I knew it was impossible to fool her. She always knew when something was up, and she would say that it wasn't always what a person said; sometimes it was what a person didn't say.

"Girl, I can hear it in your voice. And I want to know whatever it is that's bothering you. Have you prayed about it?" she repeated. I couldn't remember the last time I'd prayed, and I wasn't even going to lie.

"Honestly, I know I should be praying, but it's been awhile since I've seriously prayed about anything," I told her.

"Prayer is powerful, and prayer changes things. Always remember that. I want you to come to church with me Sunday, and bring the kids," she said. It had also been a while since I'd been in a church, but I wouldn't dare tell her no.

"Okay, we'll be there."

I knew what she was going to ask next before she even spoke. "And will that husband of yours be coming as well?" I knew that she'd never really been fond of Bryce. She'd always said there was something shifty around the eyes.

"No. It will just be the kids and me."

"Now that that's settled, do you want to talk about it?" She was concerned, and I could hear it in her voice. Right now, just the sound of her voice was having a calming effect on me. I didn't want to lose that feeling right now.

"Not yet, you know I will when I'm ready to," I told her. I knew she wouldn't push. I could come to her when I got ready to, and there was no pressure, just love.

"Okay, well, you know I'm here, so I'll just see you on Sunday."

"I love you too, and I'll talk to you later." As I hung up the phone, I noticed I wasn't shaking anymore.

The phone rang again. Looking at the caller ID, I could see it was Simone. Turning the ringer off, I left the bedroom. Simone was one of my closest friends and business partner, but I couldn't deal with her questions right now. She'd be able to tell just by the sound of my voice that something was wrong, and she'd harass me until I told her everything. I knew I was so close to breaking down that if I started talking about it, I would break and Simone would be here in five minutes.

Simone and I had met in college and we'd become fast friends. I'd needed a good friend then. Before I met Simone, it was just my son, Darren, and me in this big city. I was going to Spelman, working, and taking care of Darren. I was a young mother striving to make it, and times were not easy then. Simone and I ended up having a class together. With her bold and crazy, outgoing personality, Simone kept me laughing when I'd have otherwise been stressed. When my apartment lease ended, we decided to get an apartment together. It worked out well because we were both majoring in psychology, so we would help each other study and we would test each other and keep each other encouraged.

I went to the kitchen to get something to eat. Then I realized I wasn't even hungry anymore. I realized I did actually have to get on the phone and cancel all the reservations. I grabbed the phone in annoyance. I was really dreading this. Feeling a fresh wave of sadness come over me, I paced myself. Taking a couple of deep breaths, I calmed myself before the tears overtook me again. I refused to cry again tonight. Crying was all I seemed to do lately anyway. But I couldn't lie to myself. This really hurt.

Fifteen minutes later, after making several calls and apologizing profusely for the cancellations, I felt drained. Drained and alone. Looking around this beautiful home with all these beautiful things in it, I laughed out loud. Except the laugh really wasn't a laugh at all. To my own ears, it sounded more like the wounded cry of an animal. We'd made it, we'd gained the material things, and yet we'd lost each other along the way. We'd started off from very humble beginnings.

When I'd met Bryce, he was attending Morehouse and was already working in his field. He worked long hours but he didn't make a lot of money, so he worked a lot of overtime to earn extra money. I worked as well, but I was also still in school and basically raising Darren by myself. But back then, once we really got together, Bryce and I had been there for each other. Even though times were hard, we truly loved each other and were supportive of each other. And that's how we'd made it.

I remembered when we'd seen this house for the first time. We'd been so excited. Initially we'd talked of building our own home from the ground up, but this house was absolutely exquisite. I fell in love with the estate, which was reminiscent of a romantic southern mansion. The brick-stone mini mansion sat on sixty-two acres of land and would give us plenty of privacy and space. Our next-door neighbor practically lived eons away. The grounds had been kept perfectly with beautiful flowing gardens, and the green grass seemed to beckon Darren as he ran and jumped across the vast front yard. The inside of the home was just as stunning and beautiful as well, with huge cathedral ceilings to the dramatic winding staircase. As I walked through the halls, I could see the previous owner had added new with the old as he'd decorated the home. He'd left a few of the rooms exactly as they were. An antique room held exquisite paintings and pieces from different times and places. The library was my favorite room with its thousands of books stacked from floor to ceiling. The room was completed with two plush, taupe couches and chairs that just screamed relaxation. One of the new things was the home theater he'd had built and an indoor gym and pool. The gourmet kitchen was every chef's dream with its huge ovens and counters, with pots and pans conveniently hanging from island burners. And once Bryce had found out that the previous owner was a famous author, it was basically a done deal. I'd put aside my dream of building my own home, as this house was a dream all on its own.

With stars in my eyes, I'd thought of how we would become a family here. I was so happy then; we'd had it all. But now things were different. My husband had turned into this cold man with no feelings, and I had turned into someone I didn't even recognize anymore. I felt like some desperate woman scrambling around, trying to hold on to something that was long gone. And the more I tried to hold on, the more my husband seemed to slip away.

Maybe I should go pick up the kids, I thought to myself, but then I'd have to answer all kinds of questions from Bryce's mom. I'd taken them to her earlier, and she'd been trying to find out then what our plans for the night were. I wasn't about to tell her that I'd had to cancel our plans because her son thought a business meeting was more important than our anniversary. And the kids would ask questions as well. My daughter, Malaysia, would want to know where Daddy was and when he was coming home. My princess was ten and was just as inquisitive as ever. Darren would just give me his all-knowing look. He had just turned thirteen and knew everything there was to know in life. Darren was also my little protector. If he sensed how upset I was tonight, he wouldn't leave my side. No, I would just pick them up tomorrow, as planned.

The phone rang again. Looking at the caller ID, I saw it was Simone again. I still wasn't ready to talk to her yet, so I let the call go to voicemail. After the ringing stopped, I checked the message. "Hey, Leah, I just realized why you didn't answer my calls. Girl, you are out having a romantic evening with your husband 'cause it's your anniversary." Curling up on the couch, I settled in for a night of television. And ever so slowly, as if they had a mind of their own, the tears began again.

The earth was shaking, and I was falling. "Leah! Leah!" I woke up to see Bryce standing over me, shaking my arm. It was disgusting how my heart still skipped a beat whenever I looked at him. I still loved this man so much, but I didn't feel any love from him at all. "Are you going to work or not?" After leaving me to spend the night alone, this was all he had to say to me?

"Yes, I'm going to work. Why didn't you wake me when you came in last night?" I couldn't believe that on top of everything else, he'd let me sleep the whole night on the couch.

"Look, I was tired, so I just went to bed. Don't start with all your drama. At least I woke you up for work. And now I'm going to work." With that, he simply walked away. Rendered speechless, I could only stare as he left the house.

chapter 2

"Good morning, Dr. Gordon." It was my administrative assistant Brooke. Taking a deep breath, I gave Brooke a bright smile as I returned the greeting. I wasn't going to let my anniversary disaster affect me today. It was Monday, a new week, and I was going to start it off right. Besides, Brooke was the best. Brooke Adderly was a beautiful young woman who'd just graduated from Georgia State. When I'd interviewed her for the position, I'd known that she'd be perfect for the job. She was very intelligent, quick, and friendly. She handled the office and all the clients like an old pro. You couldn't even tell that this was her first job, and she'd only been here a year. I was so glad we'd snatched her up, even though other local practices tried to steal her away from time to time. "Dr. Gordon, your ten a.m. cancelled, but you do have Taylor Roberts at eleven."

"Thank you, Brooke. I'll be in my office if you need me." I took my case file and went to my office.

As I walked into my office, I smiled to myself. It was a room of comfort, as I liked to call it. I'd chosen soothing, earthy colors because I'd wanted my patients to feel at ease. The browns, soft yellows, and oranges blended together and created an elegant yet peaceful refuge. I still couldn't believe Simone and I had opened our own psychiatric practice, and so far been successful.

It had been a long and strenuous process. After college, we'd applied at all the same practices, and I'd gotten hired right away at the Oaklands. It was one of the most prestigious psychiatric practices in Georgia. Simone didn't get hired, and we'd been a little disappointed because we'd wanted to work together, but we celebrated my triumph with a night on the town. Not long after, Simone was hired at Winters Academy, a small but reputable practice not too far from the Oaklands. For the next several years, we worked hard and saved our money. We wanted to have our own practice one day.

I'd also had a family to consider during that time. Bryce and I had gotten married. He'd become a real father to Darren, and soon we'd had Malaysia. We were a real family. Bryce had accomplished his goals in business, and now Simone and I had our practice. It had all been so exciting, and we'd watched it grow. It was a dream come true. I just wished my home life still made me just as happy. But our home had stopped being a happy home years ago. Bryce and I had just been going through the motions for so long now. It was always the same fight over and over. He constantly worked, never having any time for me or the kids. I couldn't remember the last time we'd gone anywhere together, much less took a family vacation. The last one had been at least two years ago, and it had been the family vacation from hell. The children had fun going on all the rides, but

Bryce had moped the entire time. He got on a few rides with Malaysia, but every time I asked him to do something with me, he would just flat out say no. And it was as though he wanted us to rush through everything so we could hurry up and leave. I was miserable, and deep down I knew something was wrong.

"Dr. Gordon, Taylor is here," Brooke called. "Thank you. Send her in, please." If there was one thing that gave me true happiness, it was this. I loved helping people; that was why I'd chosen this profession in the first place. Sitting there waiting for Taylor, I mentally prepared myself to give my full concentration to my patient and block out everything else.

Taylor was a beautiful, troubled thirteen-year-old who had witnessed her father stab her mother seven times. During a heated argument, Sylver Roberts had told her husband, Tim Roberts, that she was leaving him and she wanted a divorce. Taylor had come out of her room because of the arguing. She heard her mother say that she couldn't deal with Tim's drinking anymore. And she'd told him that today was the last day that he would ever hit her again. Taylor said she'd watched her father calmly walk into the kitchen. He returned a moment later with a knife, and before either Sylver or Taylor could do anything at all, Tim Roberts had stabbed his wife seven times in the stomach. He'd then run out of the house, leaving Taylor there to watch her mother die. When the police had arrived, Taylor was sitting there, holding her mother. Covered in her mother's blood, Taylor had gone into a trance as she rocked back and forth with her mother in her arms. But when the police tried to separate her from her mother's body, she came alive instantly, fighting and scratching to hold on. The police had had to pry her away from her mother. An officer and a friend of mine, Detective Adrian Covington, had been on the scene. He said the sound of Taylor's screams had made the hairs on the back of his neck stand up.

That first time in my office, she'd been so quiet and scared I'd just wanted to hug her until the fear went away. It was true that I felt a special connection with Taylor. She'd been my first patient here at the practice, and she was the only patient who called me Dr. Leah instead of Dr. Gordon. This past year I'd helped her work through this horrifying painful experience. I heard a soft knock on the door. "Come in, Taylor." I smiled as she walked in. She was wearing a red dress, and that really spoke to me.

After her mother's funeral, Taylor had moved in with her Aunt Louise, her father's sister. Taylor had told me then that she hated leaving the house because there was so much red in the world. The color red had taken on a deep and painful meaning for Taylor. It reminded her of her mother's blood and the tragic night her mother had been stabbed to death. One day in art class, Taylor's art teacher, Mr. Williams, had shown the class a new painting he'd just purchased. The red in the picture had freaked Taylor out. She'd screamed and run out of the classroom crying uncontrollably. After that, she'd refused to go back to school. Not knowing what to do, her aunt Louise had called Taylor's uncle, Graye Barrington. Graye Barrington and Taylor's mom,

Sylver, had been fraternal twins. He was Taylor's favorite uncle, and he'd been an active part of her life from the moment she was born. From what I understood, he'd moved away four years ago. He'd talked to Taylor, and after deciding that it was just too painful for her to go to school, he decided for the time being to get a home schooling service for her. But today, here she was in my office with a red dress on.

"How are you today?" I asked her.

"I am great, Dr. Leah." Taylor spun around, showing off her red dress. "I did it. I conquered the color red." I had never seen her this happy before, and before I knew what was happening, Taylor ran around the side of my desk and hugged me. I laughed with her and returned the hug. "I owe everything to you and Uncle Graye." I noticed that she didn't say anything about her aunt Louise. I knew they hadn't been getting along lately, but I would ask her about that later. For now, I would let her bask in her happiness.

"Taylor, I am so proud of you," I told her as she went to sit and get comfortable on the couch.

"Thank you, Dr. Leah, but I couldn't have done this without you."

"Taylor, this was you. You did this, and you have come such a long way. So tell me, how does it feel to have overcome this obstacle?"

"It feels really good." Taylor stood up and spun around again. "I called Uncle Graye this morning, and I told him that red was just a color and I knew I could do this."

Looking into those happy eyes, I realized I couldn't let her diminish what she'd accomplished today. "Taylor, we both know that red was more than just a color to you. You have faced your fear and overcome it. And today you have turned the page of another chapter in your life. And that is something to really be proud of."

"Thank you for saying that, Dr. Leah. I am kind of proud of myself, and now I've got something else to tell you. Uncle Graye is moving back home!" She looked as if she would burst from excitement.

"Okay, I can tell from your facial expression how you feel about it, but tell me, how did this move come about?" I asked her.

"Well, I've been telling him for months that I wished he would come home. I mean, he's all the way in Texas. There's no family there, and he's all by himself. Dr. Leah, we used to all have so much fun together. Me, Mom, Daddy, Uncle Graye, and Aunt Carrie."

"Wait, Taylor," I said interrupting her. "I've never heard you mention an aunt Carrie before. Does she live here in Atlanta, or is she in Texas like your uncle?" I watched Taylor as sadness won over the array of emotions splaying across her face.

"Aunt Carrie was Uncle Graye's wife. She was killed in a car accident when I was eight. That's when Uncle Graye moved to Texas, and then that's when all the fun stopped. Before Aunt Carrie died, we used to have these family get-togethers with enough food to feed all of Atlanta. But my favorite part of it all was seeing my mom and Uncle Graye together. You know they were twins, and just watching them was fun. They looked so much alike. They even had the same gray eyes. They would tell all these crazy stories about when they were kids, and we would all just laugh and laugh. And it was amazing how they finished each other's sentences. When Aunt Carrie died, a lot changed. We were all sad, and Uncle Graye didn't smile at all anymore. As close as my mom and Uncle Graye were, even she couldn't put a smile on his face anymore. And then he left. My mother tried to make up for all the good times we used to have, but it just wasn't the same."

As she spoke of her uncle, my heart went out to this man who had lost so much. He'd lost his wife and now his twin sister. My own personal problems paled in comparison. "So now he's moving back within the month. I'm not sure if I told you before, but he owns a chain of construction companies. One of them is here in Atlanta, and I told him he can still run the rest of them from here. He says he misses me and he misses home. So there you go. He's coming back, Dr. Leah, and I can't wait."

Looking at her, I couldn't help getting caught up in the happiness of her moment. This was a different young lady from the one I'd seen a year ago. Her progress was phenomenal, just as the girl herself was phenomenal, and I could see she was starting to see that. As she talked, I could see a confidence in her that I hadn't seen before. "And I was thinking about going back to school, you know, real school. What do you think, Dr. Leah?"

"Taylor, I already know what you are capable of. What do you think?"

"I think I'm ready." She smiled nervously. The nervousness didn't concern me. I knew this was a big step for her. But what was most important was that she was feeling again. We concluded our session, and Taylor left my office in a very good mood.

A few moments later, there was a knock at the door, and then Simone walked in. She always did that. She would knock and then just walk in. "Hey, lady, how are you? I see your second daughter just left, and she seemed to be in good spirits." I smiled. I truly enjoyed my sessions with Taylor. "Yes, that young lady's future is looking very bright. Simone, how is your day going? Has Mr. Goodman made it in to see you today?" Mr. Goodman was one of Simone's patients, but I wouldn't say he was her favorite. He was a bald, round-shaped man who off-handedly propositioned Simone every chance he got. We were starting to think that he came to see her just for that reason alone.

"He will be here in a minute, girl. Please help me," Simone begged me.

"No, you've got this one all by yourself." I couldn't help laughing at my friend and her predicament.

"Okay, I see how you are. That's okay, but lunch will be on you today." She left my office laughing as she walked down the hall to her own office.

An hour later, Simone and I went to lunch. We decided to try this new little Italian bistro, Michelana's, that had just opened a little over a month ago. As we sat outside on the deck waiting for our lunch, I couldn't resist teasing her. "How was your session with Mr.

Goodman?" Simone rolled her eyes and playfully hit me with a napkin.

"It was semi-productive. I just have a hard time getting him to concentrate on his real issues instead of this fantasy he has of him and me. I honestly don't know what to do. I've never had to deal with this before with a patient. But enough about Mr. Goodman. How was the anniversary? Did you get my message?"

"I wish I had something to tell you, Simone, but it wasn't anything because it didn't happen." I avoided looking at her because I knew what was coming.

"Wait a minute. What do you mean 'it didn't happen'? Leah, all of those elaborate romantic plans you made. What happened?" I finally looked up at her, and I could see the concern on her face.

"He had to work late." That sounded weak even to my own ears.

"Work late!" Simone's voice was starting to rise, and I didn't want the entire restaurant to hear our conversation.

"Stop talking so loud. Yes, he had to work late, so we didn't go anywhere and we didn't do anything at all. Simone, I really don't want to talk about it right now." *As if that would stop her*, I thought to myself.

"You are a beautiful, intelligent woman but when it comes to that man, you are completely blind. How many signs do you have to see before you'll realize that there is something going on and it has nothing to do with work. This was your ten-year anniversary, and he couldn't even make time for that? That's crazy. You are a sister to me, and I love you to death, but you've got to wake up."

The waiter arrived with our food, and we sat there for a few moments in silence. Deep down, I knew she was only telling me the truth. But I wasn't ready for that kind of truth yet. I didn't know if I ever would be. "Leah, you know I would never say anything to intentionally hurt you. I just don't like the way he's treating you." Just then, Simone's cell phone rang, saving me from having to respond. "What!" Simone jumped up from the table, causing a glass of water to overturn. "You can't be serious, Brooke. Okay, okay, we're on our way. Yes, we'll be there as soon as we can." Not knowing what was going on but not liking the sound of this, I stood up and waited for Simone to get off the phone and tell me what had happened. It seemed as though she was trying to calm Brooke down. Finally, she hung up with her after promising again to get there as fast as possible. "Leah, let's go. You won't believe what Brooke just told me." Simone was practically running to the car as she talked. I had to run to catch up with her.

"What is going on, Simone? Tell me."

"Apparently, after my session with Mr. Goodman, he came back after we'd already left for lunch. When Brooke told him that I wasn't there and that he'd have to make another appointment to see me, he went ballistic. He started yelling incoherently. She said he then ran past her, up the stairs to the roof. Now he's threatening to jump off the roof to pledge his undying love for me."

Five minutes later, we arrived at the office to find the police and the fire department trying to coax Mr.

Goodman down from the roof. When Brooke saw us, she came running out of the office. "Are you okay?" Simone asked her.

"I'm fine. Well, at least better than I was, but what are we going to do? The police have been trying to talk to him, but he won't come down." I could tell that Brooke was trying to keep it together, but she was near the edge herself. I took Brooke's hand to try to calm her.

"It's going to be okay. Why don't you go ahead and go back inside? We'll take care of this. Please cancel and reschedule the rest of today's appointments." Glad to have something to do that involved some type of normalcy, Brooke went back inside.

"Simone, I need to speak with you for a moment please." It was our friend and detective Adrian Covington. We walked over to Adrian together. I was going to stay right by my friend's side. We'd never had to deal with anything like this, and this was her patient. I couldn't imagine what she was feeling right now. "Hello, Adrian. What are you doing here? You're a detective now. This isn't a murder scene." Simone was trying to make light of the situation, but I knew she was nervous. "I heard the call, and when I found out the location, I wanted to come and help. So, Simone, Joe Goodman is your patient. I know you can't go into too much detail because of doctor/patient confidentiality, but how unstable is he?"

"Well, I can give you the basics. Joe Goodman is a sixty-six-year-old widow. He lost his wife, Aimee, about six months ago. They were married for thirty-seven years. He's had a really hard time dealing with that. In the midst of all this, he seems to have developed a slight crush on me. I thought it was harmless. I never thought it would lead to something like this." Simone gestured toward the roof. We all turned to look at Mr. Goodman, who was now waving frantically and yelling something unintelligible.

"Adrian, I need to talk to Leah for a moment."

"Okay, but we don't have much time. I'll be back in a minute." Adrian walked toward the other officers. Once he was gone, Simone turned to me. "Leah, he's my patient, I have to talk him down. I know that I have to go up there, but I can't."

"Simone, what are you talking about? What's wrong?"

"Okay, I've never told you this, and please do not laugh at a time like this, but I am scared of heights." I could see the anguish on her face, and I knew she was embarrassed to admit such a thing. I couldn't help but hug her.

"Simone, I'll go. It's okay. We'll be okay. Just follow me." I took her hand, and we walked toward the building. Everyone was so busy talking they didn't notice us go inside. Once inside, I headed for the side door that led to the roof. I looked back at Simone and Brooke one last time before heading up. I smiled bravely at them. "Hey, piece of cake." As I walked up the stairs leading to the roof, I said a quick prayer to God for strength—strength for myself and Mr. Goodman.

"Hello, Mr. Goodman."

"You're not Dr. Lloyd. Where is she? And where is my Aimee?"

"Mr. Goodman, why don't you back away from the ledge so that we can talk?"

Mr. Goodman shuffled clumsily over to me and sat down on the ground. I breathed a sigh of relief. He wasn't trying to take his life or even hurt himself. He just wanted to be heard. I sat down beside him. "You know, young lady, my Aimee was a God-fearing woman. She worked hard taking care of me and our six children. She loved life and everybody in it. And she was a feisty little woman too, like Dr. Lloyd. Dr. Lloyd reminds me of my Aimee. Today made six months that my Aimee's been gone, and I just wanted to see Dr. Lloyd again, but she wasn't here. And when your secretary said she wasn't there, it was like she had left me too. Please don't think I'm crazy. I'm not crazy, it's just that the pain is hard to deal with sometimes. This morning I felt fine after I talked to Dr. Lloyd, but as the day went on, I began to feel really down, and when I came here and I couldn't talk to Aimee—I mean Dr. Lloyd, something just snapped. "Young lady, let me ask you something. Do you believe in God?" The switch in the conversation threw me off for a moment.

"Yes, I do."

"My Aimee believed in God all her life. She would rally us all together at home, you know—me, her, and the kids—for Bible study and prayer. I would fuss with her about it. I mean, she already dragged us to the Wednesday night Bible study at the church. But it was important to her, and she always said that 'a family that prays together stays together.'" That really hit home for me because I couldn't even remember the last time Bryce and I had prayed together. "I haven't prayed much since she's been gone. Aimee was always the one praying about everything. Do you think God will hear me now that she's gone?"

Mr. Goodman looked at me. I could tell he was waiting for an answer. "Personally, I think He hears us all. My grandmother Clara-Ann always says when you pray to God, His answer can come in many different ways. You just have to be open to receive it." Mr. Goodman, satisfied with my answer, continued on. "Well, I guess I can continue with the family tradition, just me and the kids. They're all married with their own kids now, but maybe just one day out of the month, we could all get together. I think my Aimee would be happy with that. And I'm also thinking that maybe this will help me deal with things better. What do you think, Doctor?"

"I think that's a very good idea, Mr. Goodman." Mr. Goodman stood up and brushed his pants off, and I stood up as well.

"Well, young lady, thank you for listening. I'm ready to go now."

"Okay yes, let's go. But let me say this to you first. Mr. Goodman, you're not crazy. You are in pain, and you have been coping the best way that you know how to. Even in pain, you reached out for help, and that is brave, Mr. Goodman."

"Yes, that is very brave." We both turned to see Simone step onto the roof. I was proud of her. "What do you say, Mr. Goodman? Let's go talk about today."

"You're still going to talk to me after all this?" he asked. Simone smiled at him. "That's what I'm here for."

The rest of the week passed by quickly and without incident. The office was back to normal. Home life was the same, just the children and me, no Bryce as usual. He'd come home late every night this week. "Hi, Mommy." Malaysia hopped into the car with a bright smile on her face.

"How was school today, baby?" I asked her. It was Friday, and I was picking her up from school.

"Let me tell you what happened to Christopher Simmons. He stuck an eraser up his nose in the middle of math facts. See we do math facts every day at eleven, but today, Mrs. Gardner said we had to switch math facts from eleven to ten because she would be leaving early today. Anyway, Mrs. Gardner was in the middle of teaching us a new problem on the black board when Christopher Simmons put an eraser up his nose. Except he shoved it too far up his nose he couldn't get it out. He started running around the classroom, and Mrs. Gardner yelled for the nurse. And then he sneezed, and the eraser flew out of his nose and it hit Lisa Parker on the forehead." I couldn't help laughing at Malaysia's expressive story.

Before I knew it, she was on to another incident that had happened during the spelling test. As I listened to her, I thought of when I'd been pregnant with her. Time had gone by so fast. It had been a really happy time then. Malaysia was expressive even then, just in a different way. She used to love to kick me all the time.

My mom said that it looked like she was doing aerobics inside my stomach. And I remembered how Bryce had been so happy about the baby. He'd been so loving and supportive, I'd felt like a queen.

"So, Mommy, can I? Please say yes." Malaysia was tugging on my sleeve.

"Say yes to what, baby?" Snapping back to the present, I realized Malaysia had asked me something. I was sure I already knew what it was. Every weekend Malaysia and her friend Sarah schemed on how they could play together. And then after they'd played for hours and hours, they'd decide between the two of them whose parents would most likely say yes if they asked to spend the night.

"Can I spend the weekend at Sarah's house?" she begged.

"Why the entire weekend, Malaysia?"

"Because tonight they're going to the movies and then we're going to have pizza. And then tomorrow is Sarah's little sister's birthday party, and I have to help them get ready for it." My child was just too much. She really didn't have to spend the entire weekend for that, but Sarah and her family lived right down the street. Plus, Malaysia's grades had been so good lately. "When your father get's home, I'll talk to him about it and then I'll let you know."

"But, Mommy, when is he coming home?" I could tell she was getting anxious.

"Soon, baby, soon." But as I pulled into our driveway, I wondered when Bryce would be home. Lately he'd been coming home later and later. I didn't really think that tonight would be any different.

"Hey, Ma!" Darren greeted me as Malaysia and I walked in, and I knew something was up right away.

"How are you?" I asked.

"I'm straight. Ma listen. Tony needs help with his chemistry project, so I was wondering if I could stay over at his place so that I can help him with it?"

Oh, my son was working me. He knew if he threw something in there about school, that I'd be more likely to say yes. "Didn't you spend the night with Tony last weekend?"

"Yes, but, Ma, this is about school, and he's gotta have this done by Monday."

"Let me talk to your father, and I'll let you know in a little while." Just then, a look flashed across Darren's face. But as quickly as the look had been there, it was gone now.

"Yeah, you have to wait just like me." Malaysia hit Darren playfully and took off running.

"Stop it, Laysia." Darren took off after her.

"Stop running through the house," I called after them.

After cooking dinner, I tried to reach Bryce again. I'd called him three times since the kids and I had come home. I'd called his office; his secretary said he'd left hours ago. His cell phone just continued to ring and ring. Slamming the phone down in frustration, I called the kids for dinner. They came running in from outside.

"Where is Daddy? Did you ask him if I could spend the weekend at Sarah's?" Malaysia wanted to know.

"Um, Daddy is working late tonight." There it was again, that look on Darren's face. "What's up Darren, why are you looking like that?" I asked him.

"Nothing, Ma. So can we go?"

"Yes, after dinner I will drop you two off." I decided to let the look issue go. During dinner, the kids kept up a steady conversation, and I seemed to be the only one who noticed that Bryce wasn't there. It had been happening so frequently lately that the children had gotten used to it, which saddened me a little, because I remembered that the first few times, they had asked a lot of questions about why Daddy wasn't home yet and why he wasn't eating dinner with us. Now it had become the norm.

After dropping the kids off, I headed back home. I'd tried to reach Bryce a few more times; now he had turned the phone off. I was getting really upset. I remembered a conversation that Simone and I had had not too long ago. I had been at her house, and I'd tried to call Bryce to ask him to pick up the kids. He'd never answered his cell phone, and I hadn't been able reach him at the office. Simone had seen the frustration on my face.

"You know, lately it's like you can never get in touch with Bryce when you need to. What's up with that?" That was Simone, she always told it like it was. There was no sugar coating anything. I'd always appreciated that in her. She was a good friend.

"Girl, I don't know. Every time I call him, he's always busy, always in a meeting, or I just can't reach him at all." I heard the tremor in my voice as I spoke. I just couldn't believe how things had changed so drastically between Bryce and me. "Leah, I have to ask you, do you think he could be having an affair?"

"No, he would never do that to me. Yes, we argue about the fact that he's always working and never has any time for me and the kids. But I know he'd never cheat on me, and he wouldn't do that to our children."

As I'd left Simone's house that day, for one split second I'd thought about what she'd said. And for one split second, I'd had this eerie feeling. Nervously laughing to myself, I'd shaken the feeling and the thought off. I hadn't truly considered the cheating notion then, and I wasn't going to tonight.

Feeling inspired, I called Bryce again. Finally he answered. "Hey, Leah, I'm kind of busy right now. Let me call you back." I didn't want to fight with him, so I didn't bring up the fact that he'd been busy all day.

"Okay, but when are you coming home? The children are spending the night with friends, and that leaves us with some alone time." I didn't like how I sounded. I could hear the desperation in my voice. I knew I was begging, but I didn't know what else to do. I was trying so hard to save us.

"Yes, I'll be home in a little while, but I have to go now." He rushed me off the phone with not so much as a good-bye or a "see you later." I refused to let that spoil everything; he was coming home. Jumping up, I headed upstairs to our bedroom. I'd never worn the lingerie I'd intended to wear on our anniversary. I smiled as I headed to the shower. I would make this a night to remember.

Slamming down the phone, I paced back and forth across the room. It was after midnight, and Bryce's be-home-in-a-little-while had turned into four hours. I could feel the anger building. He wasn't answering his phone, and I was getting sick and tired of this. What was the use of trying to save this relationship all by myself? Setting a chair right in front of the door, I decided I would sit right here in this chair until Bryce came home. He'd better be ready, because I was going to let him have it. Two hours later, I woke up stiff and tired from falling asleep in the chair. Getting up and looking outside, I realized Bryce still wasn't home. I wasn't even going to try his phone again. Feeling a serious headache coming on, I decided to lie down for a few minutes. Then I'd come right back downstairs and wait for him to come in. I was angry and tired, and I couldn't believe this was happening. Just then I heard the key turning in the door. I turned around and there he was.

"Where have you been?" I yelled. What irritated me even more was the fact that he seemed calm, like he wasn't even concerned about coming home this late.

"I told you I had to work late, don't start with the dramatics."

"You said you would be home in a little while. You didn't say anything about working this late tonight. After I didn't hear from you again, I called your office, and I was told that you'd left hours ago. Do you see what time it is? It's almost 2:30 in the morning. What is going on?" I was beyond angry, and the work excuse wasn't going to work tonight.

"You know what? I am so sick of you and your insecurities. I don't care what you were told when you called the office. I was at work, and that's all there is to it. And if you want to stand there yelling and screaming all night, that's your business, but I'm going to bed." Bryce started toward the steps. I jumped in front of him and blocked his path.

"You come home this time of night and think that you're going to sleep in *our* bed? I don't think so. You better take it to the couch." We stood there facing each other. I knew he could move me if he really wanted to, but I was ready to do battle. Suddenly he laughed.

"Do you really think I care about being in bed with *you*?" He turned and walked toward the guestroom. I was speechless. The wind had been knocked out of me. I couldn't believe he had taken it there. Who was this man? Feeling drained and humiliated, I slowly climbed the stairs to our bedroom.

chapter 3

The sound of the rain against the window startled me
awake. Sitting up in the bed, I turned on the light from
the nightstand. It was 4:45 a.m. Putting on my robe
and slippers, I went downstairs. Not able to resist, I
opened the door to the guestroom. Looking inside, I
didn't see Bryce in the bed. In fact, it looked as if the
bed hadn't been touched at all. I walked into the room
and checked the bathroom. He wasn't in there either.
"Bryce, are you in here?" Silence greeted me. Looking
out of the front door window, I could see that his car
was here. Pressing my face against the window, I looked
more closely at the car. It was pouring down rain, and
I could barely make anything out, but it looked as if
Bryce was in the car. What was he doing outside in the
rain just sitting in his car?

I raced upstairs to put my sneakers on. There was
no sense in me slipping and falling while I was outside.
I ran back downstairs. When I looked out the window
again, I saw that he was still sitting there in the car.
Not wanting him to see me yet, I silently crept outside
through the glass sliding doors on the side of the house.
Feeling the rain and the wind blowing, I quickly walked

around the side of the house until I found myself right behind Bryce's car. I walked to the driver's side, and I could feel the butterflies in my stomach. I became oblivious to the rain. The nervous feeling increased as I stood there looking at Bryce through the window. He was talking on his cell phone, and he was so engrossed in his conversation that he didn't even see me. I could tell by his gesturing and smiling that it wasn't an argument. Something just wasn't right about this. He laughed out loud, a deep sensuous laugh, and that was all I could take.

I yanked open the door, letting the rain and the wind in the car. "What are you doing? Who are you talking to?" He sat there in surprise, but guilt was written all over his face. "Answer me, Bryce. Who are you talking to?"

"Baby, this is my mom." There was no way that he would laugh like that with his mother.

"Okay, let me speak to your mom." Before he had a chance to react, I snatched the phone out of his hand. "Hey, Mom," I said into the phone.

"Leah, give me my phone." Bryce got out of the car and made a grab for the phone. I backed away from the car. "I can't hear you, *Mom*. Are you there?" The anger inside grew as I could hear the person on the other end of the line breathing and not saying a word. Just then, Bryce moved forward and snatched the phone from me.

"I have to go," he told the person on the other end. I stood there in disbelief. I slowly walked up to him. I was so angry I felt outside of myself, and before I knew it, I slapped Bryce in the face as hard as I could.

He grabbed me, and for a moment I thought he would hit me back, but I wasn't scared. In this moment, I was ready for anything. I felt so out of control. Looking into his face, I could see he was fighting for control as well. He let go of me, turned around, and headed toward the house. "I want you out, right now."

He stopped and faced me again. "Where am I supposed to go this time of night? Look, you need to calm down. She's just a friend." The verbal confirmation that it was a she gave me a sick feeling and threatened to send me over the edge again.

"Since when do you come outside at five in the morning to talk to a friend on your cell phone? In the pouring rain? Are you serious? What could you possibly have to talk about?" He just stood there with this stupid look on his face. I wanted to slap him again. "Like I said, I want you out. I don't care where you go, but I want you out of this house."

"You can't put me out of my own house." He started walking back toward the house.

"Bryce, try me if you want to. I'll call the police and get the news people out here. There will be a scene like you've never seen before. Now how would it look for the owner of one of the biggest real estate companies in Georgia to be splashed all over the news for a domestic dispute?" He'd always been concerned with his image. And I was right, that stopped him right in his tracks. "So go ahead, try me," I told him.

"Let me get some clothes."

"No, you wait here. I'll get the clothes." I walked past him and into the house. I locked the door behind me even though I knew he had his keys. In a daze, I grabbed some of his things. I walked toward the front door and felt my anger building again. I opened the door and threw his clothes at him. As he scrambled to catch them, I slammed the door and locked it again.

Falling to the ground right there in the foyer, I began to cry uncontrollably. I felt like I was dying inside. I'd never experienced pain like this before, and it rocked me to my absolute core. He hadn't admitted anything, but deep down inside I knew he was cheating on me. All I could do was lie there on the ground and cry hysterically. After a long while, the crying turned to whimpering. Finally, finding enough strength to drag myself to the living room, I collapsed on the couch. I don't know how or when, but sleep finally began to claim me. As I drifted off, I had one last thought: *This night has changed everything, and my life will never be the same again.*

A few hours later, I was awakened by the sound of birds chirping and the sunlight peeping through my curtains. The familiar sounds, and even the fact that the sun was shining, were a total contradiction of how I was feeling. Attempting to ignore the birds, the sun, and just life in general, I turned over in the bed away from the windows. Big mistake. Now I was facing the empty space where Bryce would have normally been. In ten years, we'd never slept a night apart. Angrily brushing away tears, I jumped up from the bed.

The sound of the telephone ringing startled me. I felt butterflies in my stomach as I looked at the caller ID and realized that it was Bryce. Pacing back and forth across the room, I tried to decide whether or not I should answer the phone. On one hand, I just wanted to rip the phone out of the wall and throw it out the window. On the other, I had to know for sure. I had to hear him say it. I reached for the phone just as the ringing stopped. I sat down on the bed to calm my nerves. Maybe it was for the best. Maybe I just wasn't ready to handle this right now.

The phone began ringing again, and I just stared at it for a moment. It was Bryce again. Ready or not, I just had to know the truth. Taking a deep breath, I answered the phone. "For once, tell me the truth. Are you having an affair?"

"Leah, baby, listen."

"No!" I shouted into the phone. I had started off calm, but I felt myself about to go over the edge again. "I just want the truth. You owe me that. Just tell me, are you having an affair?" It seemed like a lifetime passed before he answered.

"Yes," With that one simple word, he turned my world upside down. "Leah, listen. Yes, I cheated, but, baby, it's over with her." I felt like I was going to be sick.

"Is that supposed to make me feel better, the fact that you say it's over?" I screamed. "How could you do this to me? How could you do this to our family?" I slammed the phone down and ran to the bathroom. Once in the bathroom, I splashed cold water over my face. I closed my eyes and took a deep breath. The sick feeling had gone away but I still felt light-headed. I went and sat down on the corner of the bed.

For years I'd counseled women and men on this same issue, adultery. And even though my heart went out to my patients, I'd always been able to be objective and keep a professional distance. But this wasn't a patient; this was me. There was no way to be professional about this because the simple truth was my heart was breaking and there was no escaping this feeling, this moment. I felt out of control. I couldn't believe this was happening to *me*. Sobbing and screaming, I slid from the edge of the bed onto the floor. This was too much. The pain was almost unbearable. For the first time in my life, I didn't have the answers. And there were so many emotions all at once. One minute I was screaming and crying, and the next I'd feel this numbness come over me. While screaming and crying, I felt consumed with rage; in the numbness, I just felt nothing. It was as if I were shutting down. What was I going to do? How could I make it through this? I was lost and I couldn't find myself. Sensing movement within the room, I turned to see Bryce standing in the bedroom door. In that moment, I hated him. I hated him for doing this to me, and I hated him for seeing me like this.

"Leah, we need to talk." Ignoring his outstretched hand to help me up off the floor, I got up and went to stand by the window. Just a moment ago I'd hated him. Now I was just hurt. It felt like too much pain for one person to deal with.

"How long has this been going on, Bryce?" I was surprised at how calm my voice sounded.

"Why does that matter when I already told you that it's over? Look, I know you're hurt and everything, but I mean, this isn't all my fault. I mean, we haven't been getting along for a long time now, and last year you were the one that mentioned divorce."

I turned away from the window to face him now. "Are you serious? Is that the best you can do? After ten years of marriage, that's the best you can come up with? We haven't been getting along, and yes, in the middle of a heated argument—which, by the way, was over a year ago—I said the word *divorce*. And you think that gives you the right to go out and sleep with another woman. Who is she, Bryce?"

"She's no one. Look, I didn't come here to argue about this. It's over, and that's all there is to it. You need to really let this go." *I can't believe him! He isn't even apologetic. And he expects me to just let it go? Does he think he's going to get away with this?* "I said who is she, Bryce? You're crazy if you think you're going to just come in here with these lame excuses and your big announcement that it's over with her and that's going to make what you did okay."

"Okay, you want truth? Here it is, and you'd better be ready for it."

"Her name is Angela Walters, and I met her a year ago. Let's see, what else do you want to know? She's young, beautiful, and she owns her own business. And oh yes, the sex is great." Rage as I had never known it before, took control of me. Screaming and crying, I flew at him from across the room, slapping and hitting him. Trying to get at him any way I could, I continued to hit him. Consumed with rage, I ripped his shirt off. I wanted him to hurt the way I hurt. All I could think of was revenge. Bryce grabbed me and began choking me. I slapped and scratched at his hands. Slamming me up against the wall, Bryce finally let go.

Choking and coughing, I struggled to catch my breath. I sat down on the bed, and Bryce sat next to me. Just moments ago, we had been screaming and fighting. Now there was just silence. In the eleven years that we'd been together, it had never come to this. We'd never put our hands on each other. Looking into his eyes, I could see he was just as shocked as I was. I couldn't stand to be near him. I went and stood by the window again. "Please go, Bryce."

"But, Leah—"

"No, Bryce, I need you to leave, please. I want some time alone. I don't want to argue or fight anymore. I am asking you to please leave." I looked him in the eyes, wanting him to see how serious I was. Without saying another word, Bryce left the room. It wasn't long before I heard the sound of his car as he drove away.

A few minutes later, I heard the doorbell ring. I drifted downstairs toward the front door in a daze. It was Simone. I opened the door and practically collapsed in her arms. "Honey, what's wrong? What happened? I've been calling you all morning, and I kept getting a busy signal. Something just didn't feel right, so I decided to come over here." She wiped my tear-stained cheeks. "Leah, what happened? You know I'm here for you. You can tell me anything. Looking up at her, I tried to find the words to say. "It's okay, I'll wait. You can talk when you're ready."

After a few minutes, I finally had the strength to talk. "You were right all along, Simone. He *is* cheating on me. Her name is Angela Walters, and the sex is great apparently."

"Leah, tell me he didn't say that to you. Please tell me he didn't."

"Yes, he did, and then we actually fought. When he said that, I lost it. I went absolutely crazy. I attacked him."

"You attacked him?"

"Yes, I ran at him like I was on the football field." We looked at each other and laughed. I couldn't believe we were laughing, but I couldn't believe a lot of things that were happening lately.

"I'm sorry. It really isn't funny, but I just had a mental picture of you attacking Bryce, and I just never imagined you attacking anyone, much less Bryce. So how did you leave things? Do you need me to make a phone call. You know I know some people, right? Girl, what do y—"

"Simone, slow down. And no, don't call anyone. There has been enough fighting."

"Are you sure, girl, because I know somebody who can break him down." My friend was crazy. I couldn't help but laugh. One minute she was a brilliant psychologist, and the next she was home girl from the hood. But I loved that about her. Despite her success, she never forgot where she came from, and she could switch back and forth in a New York minute, depending on the situation at hand.

"Yes, I am sure Simone. Thanks, but no thanks."

"So who is she? Is she someone we know?" Simone stopped speaking for a moment to give me a serious look. "I am so sorry. I'm being completely insensitive. Do you even want to go into all of this?"

"It's okay. I need to talk to someone before I explode again. Honestly, Simone, I still feel like I'm in shock. I can't believe he had an affair. I can't believe we actually fought. How could this happen?" Not knowing what to do with the emotions that were swirling inside of me, I stood up and began pacing around the room. "He said her name, but who is she really? Does she know he's married? And more importantly, what is she doing for him that his wife of ten years couldn't do? Now he says it's over with her, though. Does he really expect me to believe that? He's been lying all this time, so what else is he hiding?" I stopped pacing for a moment and looked at my friend as if she had the answers, even though I knew deep down she didn't. In the midst of all these unanswered questions was this gnawing increasing need to actually see Angela Walters. For some insane reason I wanted to know everything about her. "Simone, I want to see her. I want to know what she looks like. I have to know."

"Leah, I don't think that's a good idea." I looked at her in surprise.

"Just a minute ago, you were talking about breaking Bryce down. What's changed?"

"That was before. I'm thinking clearer now. And I've never seen you like this before. You're starting to make me nervous. I mean, seriously, Leah, I am worried about you. What if finding out everything and seeing her drives you over the edge?" I stopped pacing and sat down on the couch next to Simone.

"Look, Bryce came in here today and said that the affair is over, but I don't believe a single word that comes out of his mouth. I have to face this thing head-on. It's driving me crazy not knowing everything. And I don't know what's going to happen with Bryce and me. All I know is that I need the truth. Simone, you know practically everyone in Atlanta. There has to be someone who can find this Angela Walters."

"You know I will help you in any way I can. I'm just worried about you. Once we start this, there is no turning back. And whatever we find out, I just want to know that you can handle it, that you're going to be okay." I knew she was concerned about me, but I couldn't make any promises about anything.

"To be honest, I'm not really handling anything about this situation right now. And I'm not okay. My emotions are all over the place. I don't know what to do. The only thing I am sure of is that I need truth. I mean, seriously, would you not want to know?"

"Okay, point taken." Simone stood up and walked over to the phone. I had knots in my stomach already, and we hadn't even found out anything yet.

Simone turned to look at me as she spoke on the phone. "Hello, Adrian, I have a favor to ask you. I remember you used to have this private detective friend that you used to always hang out with. Do you still talk to him?" Simone laughed suddenly. "No, I am not interested in him. Leah and I are trying to find out some information about someone. Yes. Her name is Angela Walters. Okay, okay, just call him for me, and call me back when you know something. Bye, Adrian." Simone was still laughing as she hung up the phone. "So Adrian will call us when he knows something."

Attempting to hide my nervousness, I changed the subject. "What made you call Adrian, and how do you know who he used to hang out with?"

"Well, Adrian is our friend, so who better to call than a friend who's a cop and knows how to track people down. I'd forgotten Adrian's friend's name. It's Sean Gregory. "Okay yes, I have actually heard of him. They say he is the best in Atlanta. When you need to know who, what, when, and where, he is the one to go to. But you're still not answering my question. How do you know who Adrian hangs out with?" I looked at her expectantly. She paused before answering.

"Okay, fine. But there's really not much to tell. About a year ago, Adrian and I went out on a few dates. I have to admit we had fun. It was never serious, and you know I would have told you if I felt it was really going somewhere."

I playfully threw a pillow at her. "And why didn't it last? What happened? Spill it. I know there is more to this story."

"I mean, we had a lot of fun. But that was not too long after I ended things with Chris, so we just remained friends. And you, young lady, are lucky I love you so much." Simone playfully threw the pillow back at me.

"Why is that?" I asked her.

"Because I had to agree to dinner with Adrian for him to help us."

"Oh, you know you want to go anyway." Simone couldn't hide the smile peeking from the corners of her mouth. "Girl, you know me too well. I can't wait to go." We both laughed then. It felt good to laugh.

"So where are the kids?"

"They are both spending the weekend with friends. Originally, it was only supposed to be Malaysia, but you know Darren knows how to work his mama. Anyway, I'm glad they weren't here to witness all this craziness. And knowing Darren, he would have tried to jump in, and it just wouldn't have been a good situation at all."

"You're right about that because I'd hate to have to hurt Bryce over my godson."

"So what do we do now?"

"We just have to wait. That's all we can do at this point. I know one thing, though: you are going to eat something, because I know you haven't." I smiled as we headed toward the kitchen. I wasn't hungry, but knowing Simone, she would make sure I ate everything on my plate.

Hours later, we were settled in the living room talking when we heard the phone ring. I walked over to the phone, and when I saw it was Adrian, I handed the phone over to Simone. I was just too nervous. I wanted to know more than anything what he'd found, if anything, but I was also scared about what the truth would reveal. I went to sit down on the couch as Simone talked to Adrian. "Yes. Okay. Uh-huh. Wait just one second." Simone gestured for me to get her something to write with. I hurried to get her a pen and piece of paper. "Okay, shoot." Simone was all business now as she began to write frantically. "Okay. Uh-huh. Yes." If I heard her say "okay" or "uh-huh" one more time, I was going to scream. The suspense was killing me. As I sat there, I tried to calm myself by thinking good thoughts, which would have been great if I'd had any good thoughts. Who was I kidding? I couldn't think of anything right now except the fact that Simone was on the phone finding out information about the other woman in my husband's life. "The other woman," I said to myself out loud. It sounded so strange to me. *And who is really the other woman? Is it Angela Walters, or is it me*, I wondered.

Finally, after what seemed like an entire lifetime, Simone hung up with Adrian and walked over to the couch. As she sat down next to me, I glanced at the paper she'd written on. It seemed to go on forever. She sighed as she looked at me. "Okay, let's both take a deep breath. Are you ready to hear this?" I took a deep breath.

"As ready as I'll ever be."

"Okay, in three hours, Adrian and Sean Gregory were able to find out a lot about Ms. Angela Walters. Well, I guess we should say Mrs. Angela Walters. She's married. Angela and her husband, Corey Walters, were high school sweethearts. They separated four years ago. Simone stopped talking and stood up. She began to pace as I'd done earlier. I had never seen my friend this nervous, and in turn, my own hands began to shake. What was she going to tell me that could be worse than what I'd already learned? Whatever it was, there was no since in delaying it any further. "Please tell me what it is. I really need to know." Simone sat down again and looked at me nervously. "I'm going to tell you. I just needed to take a moment. It really isn't easy for me, because I know you're going to be even more hurt than you are now." She took a deep breath and began again. "Girl, brace yourself. Angela Walters and Bryce have been seeing each other for three years. So there's one lie since he told you he met her a year ago."

Three years! He's been seeing another woman for three years, and I had no idea. My marriage has been a lie! The room began to spin as the truth sank in. Suddenly feeling nauseous, I jumped up and ran to the bathroom. In the bathroom, I immediately turned on the faucet and started splashing my face with water. In the distance, I could hear Simone knocking on the door asking me if she could come in. Instead of answering, I opened the door so she could see that I was okay. She didn't try to talk to me, and I was grateful for that. After a few moments, the nausea subsided and I attempted to pull myself together mentally. Breathing evenly again, I turned and faced her.

"There's more, isn't there?

"Yes, there is."

"Okay, I am ready. Let's go back to the living room. I turned the bathroom light off and followed her back to the couch to sit down.

"Are you sure you're okay now?"

"Yes, I need to know everything so I can try to begin to deal with this."

"Okay, he is still seeing her. Sean didn't just get information for you; he tailed Mrs. Walters, and…" Simone looked away as her voice trailed off.

"What, Simone? Tell me. I have to know."

She sighed as she continued on. "They were seen coming out of the Wyndam Hotel." Pain sliced through me as I imagined my husband with this woman. I held up my hand. I needed Simone to just give me a moment. So he was still lying to me. He'd gone to her after coming here and telling me that he'd ended it with her. It wasn't that I'd even believed him as he'd stood there claiming it was over. Deep down I'd known better. But having my suspicions confirmed didn't make it any easier to deal with. "Sorry, Leah."

"Is there anything else?" I asked my friend. Simone looked down at her notes. "Yes, you won't believe this, she only lives fifteen minutes away from here. I have her home address and cell phone number."

"What does she do?" It was such a lame question, but I didn't know what else to ask. There was just so much to process. "She owns an art gallery called Soul Expressions. There is a seven o'clock showing there tonight." Simone handed me the paper, and I reached for the phone.

I'd already found out more than I expected, but I still wanted to know if she even knew he was married with children. Looking at her number, I just knew I couldn't resist calling it. My heart was beating fast as I blocked my phone number from showing and dialed Angela Walters' cell phone. On the fourth ring, someone picked up. But it wasn't Angela's voice I heard on the other end. It was my husband's. "Hello," he said impatiently several times.

I froze. The phone slipped from my hands and fell to the floor. "What happened?" Simone grabbed the phone and redialed. I heard her say hello. A moment later she slammed the phone down. "He hung up on me. Do you think he might have recognized my voice?" I looked at her sadly and shrugged.

"I have no idea." We sat in silence for a while, looking at each other. We were both at a loss for words. I closed my eyes. I was trying so hard to keep it together. Simone walked over and hugged me, and then I broke down. I cried for me, I cried for my children, and I cried for the family that I'd thought we were. I'd been prepared to speak to Angela Walters. I'd even accepted the fact that things might get ugly on the phone. I should have prepared myself for anything, but I hadn't. Hearing Bryce answer the other woman's phone only added to the pain of this horrific nightmare.

I sat there in silence for a while, and more than ever, I appreciated my friendship with Simone. She didn't press me to talk or to do anything at all. She moved about the house, clearing the dishes we'd used for lunch and leaving me to my thoughts. I just needed some time right now; time to at least try to sort through some of this mess in my mind. At this point, I had no idea what to do about anything. My entire world had been pulled out from underneath me.

After calling both kids to check on them, I went in search of Simone. I smiled as I thought of Malaysia and Darren. At least they were having a good time. But most importantly, they had no idea what was going on at home. So at least for right now, I didn't have to worry about them and how all of this was going to affect them. I wanted to shield my children and protect them from this nightmare, but I had no idea how I was going to do that.

chapter 4

I finally found Simone in the library. She was so engrossed in the novel she was reading that initially she didn't even notice me enter the room. Walking further into the room, I smiled as I looked around. The library was still one of the things I loved most about this house. It was historically traditional, with books lined up on shelves from the ceiling to the floor. There was so much to choose from with the genres, ranging from romance to science fiction. I hadn't really changed anything except for the two plush couches that made it more comfortable than the stuffy chairs that were originally here. Simone turned around once she heard me. "How are you feeling?" I could see the concerned look on her face.

"I honestly don't know. I am feeling so many different things right now. I don't know whether I am coming or going." I sat down on the plush sofa and tried to get comfortable. Simone left the shelves of books to come sit across from me on the other couch.

"You know, for the first time in my life, I feel completely lost. I mean, Bryce and I have had problems yes, but I always assumed that we'd work them out together. I've been so naïve thinking that him having an affair was something I'd never have to worry about. I should've seen the signs. I guess I just didn't want to see. I remember that one day you tried to tell me, but I wouldn't even listen." Simone held up her hand to stop me from going on.

"Don't do this to yourself. Leah, no wife wants to believe her husband is cheating. I don't care what kind of problems there might be in the marriage. Whatever the two of you are going through, that still doesn't give him the right to do what he's doing."

"That's it. Let's go," I said, standing up. Simone looked confused for a moment. I gave her a knowing look, and when she realized what I was talking about, she stood up as well. "We're going to that art showing tonight, aren't we?"

"Yes."

"You know I'll go with you, but are you sure you want to do this?" Closing my eyes, I thought of all that had happened today. Bryce had had a chance to come clean, lay everything out on the table, but still he'd lied. He was still sleeping with her. And I couldn't erase the memory of hearing him answer Angela's phone. It was how he'd sounded that devastated me the most. His voice had been happy and carefree as if he hadn't a care in the world. How dare he humiliate me like this. Looking at Simone, I made up my mind.

"No, I'm not sure, but I'm going anyway."

Hours later, I stood before the mirror. I'd tried on four dresses, and I was still undecided. Simone walked in looking absolutely gorgeous in an off-the-shoulder, mahogany, cashmere sweater peppered with gold sequins. And the razor-cut mahogany pants fit to perfection. I had to smile. My friend had curves that went on for days, and when she walked in the room, you knew she knew it. "If Mr. Goodman could see his Dr. Lloyd now," I teased her. Simone laughed.

"Leave my patient alone, he is making real progress now."

"Seriously, Simone, I am glad to hear that. Mr. Goodman has been dealt some really hard blows. I was hoping that he'd come around."

"Yes, I am glad too. Now what is going on with you? It's going to take us at least forty minutes to get there. What's the hold up?" Frowning, I looked at myself in the mirror again.

"I don't know. I can't decide on anything." Simone came and stood behind me.

"Leah, look at yourself. You are wearing that dress, and you know it. You could rock a t-shirt and jeans and still look beautiful." Looking in the mirror, I knew I looked good on the outside, but for the first time in my life, I didn't feel good on the inside. Simone turned me around until I was facing her. "I know what this is really about. Bryce has really shaken some things up inside of you; I know that. But don't ever let him shake your confidence in yourself. You've never doubted yourself in that aspect, and you're not going to start now. So if we're going to do this, let's find you some shoes and let's get this show on the road."

We arrived at the art show at 7:20 p.m., and from the looks of things, the show was in full swing. Looking around the parking lot, I could see there were a lot of people here. I took a deep breath to get my nerves together. Maybe this wasn't such a good idea. I turned to Simone to tell her that I wanted to leave. "Simone, I think we—" I stopped talking when I realized she wasn't listening. I followed her gaze, and then I saw him. It was Bryce. We sat there in the car and watched as he walked across the street and entered the building.

Simone looked at me. "No he didn't."

"Yes, he did. Let's go," I told Simone as I got out of the car and began walking toward the building. There was no way I was leaving now. This was something I had to see. *Lord, please give me strength.*

Once inside, I had to admit it was amazing. It was clear to see that whatever else Angela Walters may be, she was definitely talented. And had this been under different circumstances, I would have been able to enjoy the powerful and beautiful black art displayed before me. Simone and I walked through the crowd, but we didn't see any sign of Bryce or Angela. There were so many people there. "Everyone, can I have your attention, please." The crowd moved and made room for Angela Walters as she took center stage. So here she was, the woman my husband was having an affair with. Simone gave my shoulder a light squeeze. I smiled at her slightly to let her know that I was okay, even though we both knew I wasn't. Turning my attention back to center stage, I studied the woman standing before me.

She was cute enough, in a girl-next-door kind of way, although her figure was more boyish than wom-anly. "The sex is great." My knees almost buckled as my mind flashed back to Bryce's statement. I tried to concentrate on what Angela Walters was saying. "I want to thank you all for coming out tonight, it has been a true success. And to join in the celebration with us, we have a special guest. Everyone, please welcome and put your hands together for my business partner and friend, Mr. Bryce Gordon." *Business partner?* As the applause began, Bryce appeared and stood beside Angela. Pain shot through my entire body as I watched them stand there together. All around me, I saw happy faces and people clapping. This was a happy occasion for them. But there was nothing for me to celebrate. Here was the man I'd spent most of my adult life with. The man I'd married and raised a family with. The man I'd believed in. The man I loved.

"Leah, I'm getting you out of here." Simone pulled on my arm, but I couldn't move. I couldn't take my eyes off the two of them. For the second time today, I felt like I was outside of myself. "Leah, listen to me, please." The sound of Simone's voice snapped me out my daze. When I looked at her, I could see she was near crying. Simone never cried. The next thing I knew, I was crying. "I am not going to stand here and tell you that I know what you're going through right now. This hurts me, and it's not even happening to me. All I know is that we need to leave now. Nothing good will come out of this if we stay. I know what I said earlier today about breaking Bryce down, but I am thinking of you now. You and the kids. He is not worth it, Leah. Please, let's go." She grabbed my hand and pulled me toward the door.

As we walked away, I turned to look at them one last time, and my eyes locked with Angela Walters's. She gasped and stumbled when she realized who I was. *She knows who I am. She knows he's married.* Angela turned and ran from the room while Bryce looked around, trying to see what Angela was running from. As his gaze settled on me, he froze. I took a step toward him, but Simone was too fast for me. She grabbed me and pushed me through the door.

Once outside, the cool wind hit my face, causing me to step back. Simone, taking the step back as a sign that I was trying to go back inside, tightened her grip as she led me across the parking lot to the car. When we reached the car, I leaned against the door. My head was spinning, and I felt dizzy. Simone was about to get in the car. When she saw the condition that I was in, she rushed around to my side of the car.

She opened the passenger door. "Leah, sit down. You look like you're going to pass out. Please don't pass out on me." As I sat down, I looked up at her. For the third time today, I could see concern written all over her face.

"How could he do this, Simone? And did you hear what she said? Business partner. So not only are they sleeping together, but they're in business together too?"

"Leah, I honestly don't know what to say. I mean, this whole night feels like a Lifetime movie." We looked at each other for a moment. I could tell by the expression on her face that she thought she might have gone too far with that last statement. I laughed, and then we were both laughing. It wasn't long before my laughter turned to tears.

"Let's just go, I need to get away from here." I had been sitting on the edge of the seat with the passenger door open. I swung my legs around until I was back in the car, and then I shut the door. Simone walked around the car to the driver's side and got in.

"Where do you want to go?" she asked me.

"I don't know, let's just ride wherever."

For the next hour and a half we rode all over Atlanta, listening to India Arie CDs. I'd always loved her music. It was so alive and pure. I just felt free listening to her. Her voice was absolutely incredible. It completely captivated me. As "I Am Ready for Love" began to play, I stopped the CD. It had always been one of my favorite songs by her, but I just couldn't handle it tonight. Simone switched CDs and popped in the new Mary J. Blige, my other favorite singer. I'd grown up with her, and her voice was in a class all by itself. It was so real and soulful. Her words always hit home for me. Whether it was a song about love or pain, it was as if she always knew exactly what I was going through.

We rode a little while longer in silence, until I began to feel the tiredness taking over. "Simone, I think I'm ready to go home now." I couldn't imagine myself going to sleep, but my body seemed to have a mind of its own.

As Simone pulled into my driveway, memories flooded my mind. I thought of the first day we'd moved into this house. We'd been so happy to finally have our own home. The kids had also been excited. They rushed from the car to explore their new yard and home. Bryce and I had just stood there for a moment, holding hands and looking at our new home. "Baby, we did it." I remembered Bryce squeezing my hand then. I'd felt so connected to him.

"Yes, baby, we did," I said, squeezing his hand back as we walked up the steps to our home.

"Leah, hello. Calling Leah." Simone snapped me out of memories from the past.

"I'm sorry girl, I was somewhere else."

"I was asking if you'd like me to stay with you. I know you're picking the kids up in the morning, but I just don't think you should be by yourself. Hey, we can rent some movies, get some popcorn, and have a girls' night." She was trying so hard to take my mind off things, and I loved her for it, but right now I just wanted to be alone.

"Simone, I don't think I'll be good company tonight, but I'll call you a little later." I hugged her as I got out of the car.

"Are you sure?" she asked.

"Yes, I'm sure. I don't even know how to thank you for everything. You are such a good friend to me, and you have really been there for me. I just need some time."

"Okay, well, I will call and check on you. And you don't need to thank me. You would have done the same for me." She was right. Had the roles been reversed, I would have. She waved as she drove off. I turned around and walked toward the house. It was empty in more ways than one. I walked into the dark home, knowing that Bryce wouldn't be showing up tonight. There was no way that he was going to face me tonight. But for once, I was glad that he wouldn't be here because honestly, he was the last person I wanted to see right about now. I was so out of control of my emotions, I knew that seeing him now would drive me straight over the edge.

I was exhausted. I hadn't slept well in days, and I was starting to feel delirious. I climbed the stairs to my bedroom. Flipping on the light, I saw the dresses I'd tried on before Simone and I had left for the art gallery. They were everywhere—on the bed, strewn across my lounge chair, a few had even fallen to the floor. I needed to clean this mess up, but I just didn't have the energy. *This will just have to wait until morning.* Flipping the light off, I walked over to the bed in the darkness. I sat down and took my shoes off. As I threw on my nightgown, I felt my body shutting down before my head even hit the pillow.

Sometime after midnight, the phone rang, jarring me awake. "Hello," I said groggily.

"It's me, Granny." Instantly I remembered I was supposed to go to church with her in the morning. Well, she was going to be disappointed, because I wasn't going anywhere except to pick up the children and bring them home. "Hey, I just wanted to make sure you remembered about church tomorrow."

"I don't think I'll be able to make it. I'm not feeling very well." I wasn't about to go into everything with her tonight, even though I knew I was giving such a weak excuse for not going.

"Once you get to church you'll feel much better, because Jesus is the number-one doctor. Besides that, my ride cancelled on me, so you're the only other option I have. So I'll see you here at my house at ten a.m. sharp. I love you. Bye."

And with that, she hung up the phone. I tried to call her right back, but now her phone was busy. She'd seen right through me and my excuse. She knew me so well. And she also knew that I wasn't going to leave her stranded without a way to church. As I drifted off to sleep again, I had the sneaking suspicion that I'd been played by Granny tonight.

"I am so glad you came today." My grandmother smiled and hugged me and the children again for the second time today. I could tell she really was happy that we were here. When I'd gone to pick her up, she'd been standing on the side of the curb and practically jumped in the car when I drove up. But coming to church this morning had been a real struggle for me. I hadn't really wanted to go anywhere, but I didn't see that I had had any other choice, because I couldn't leave her stranded. *But now that we are here, I might as well make the best of it,* I silently told myself. We followed Granny down the aisle, and I saw some familiar faces. It had been a few years since I'd been here at Blessed Life Baptist Church. To my left was Mrs. Fowler. She waved when she saw me, although I wouldn't have missed her in that hot pink dress. She also had a huge hot pink hat and purse to match. Mrs. Fowler had always been known for wearing the brightest colors. *Some things never change*, I thought.

Looking over to my right, I saw the Roberson twins. I'd gone to school with them as children, and we'd also attended Harrington Winds High School together as well. As children, the twin girls had always dressed alike and did everything together. I saw that hadn't changed much either; they were wearing matching pants suits. As if on cue, they both waved and smiled at me at the exact same time. *How do they do that?* I waved back as we continued down the aisle. I hoped and prayed that Granny wasn't going to have us sit on the front row. It was bad enough that all eyes were on us, but leave it to her to put us right on front row. Sighing, I put on a smile. *I should've just stayed in bed.*

Finally, Granny stopped a few pews short of the first row. Lo and behold, she sat us right next to Rain Howard, "mouth of the south." We said hello to each other as I sat down next to her. Personally, I didn't have anything against Rain. I hadn't seen her in years. She was another former classmate. We'd played on the same volleyball team in high school and even attended the same church. I remembered growing up in that church with Rain, and there had been many arguments and fights over something she'd said or thought she'd heard. She'd always lived up to her name because most of the time when Rain came around, a storm was sure to follow. I hadn't see her in years. Maybe she'd changed. Shrugging my shoulders, I turned to face the choir as they began to sing "Blessed Assurance." Even if she hadn't changed, I was not going to get involved with her foolishness today. I had my own drama to deal with.

Despite my efforts to ignore her, it wasn't long before Rain was nudging me in my side. "Girl, who is he? Look, he is absolutely delicious." Inwardly groaning to myself, I once again attempted to ignore her. But she wasn't having any of that. Next she elbowed me. "Leah, look. You've got to see this." *She just isn't going to stop.* Turning to see what she was hyperventilating about, I looked into the eyes of the most beautiful man I'd ever seen, and instantly I felt myself drowning in deep pools of gray. I'd never seen eyes like his before. Seconds passed as our eyes locked, forming a connection that went beyond anything I'd ever felt before in my life. *Oh, this is crazy. How can I have a connection with a complete stranger? I've never even seen him before. I must be losing my mind.* Not understanding what was happening inside, I was the first to look away. "Do you know him?" Nothing got past Rain.

"No, I don't know him, Rain."

"Well, it sure looks like you know each other to me."

"Well, we don't, so drop it." Determined to block out Rain and the new mysterious man, I faced the choir once again.

I felt so ashamed when I realized the music had stopped and Pastor Richards was making church announcements. He was saying something about the annual church picnic. For the next few minutes, he went over some of the activities that would take place at the picnic. It really sounded like fun. *Fun.* I couldn't remember the last time I'd truly had any. Rain leaned over to whisper, "He's got to be at least six foot three, and that skin, girl, like hot caramel melting in your mouth. Those eyes and that body, mm mm mm." *Okay, that's it. We are both going to hell.* I refused to even respond to Rain's comments. I did my best to concentrate on what Pastor Richards was saying.

"Now, if we can please have all of our youth between the ages of twelve and nineteen come down, please. Parents, we have something special for the kids today."

Darren looked at me expectantly. "Ma, can I go?"

"Go ahead, Darren. But behave yourself."

Granny leaned across Malaysia. "They also have children's church. Why don't you let Darren take Malaysia down, and then they can both have fun." I looked at Malaysia. Her eyes were pleading with me to say yes.

"Okay, you can both go. Just remember what I said about behaving." They both took off after all the other kids. Within minutes, all the children had gone to have a good time in Jesus's name.

"You know, I had my sermon all planned out for today," said Pastor Richards. "Here it is." He waved some papers in the air. "It was prepared and studied, and I was ready to preach this sermon. But as the choir sang, the Lord spoke to me."

Rain waved her hand in the air. "Amen, Pastor, speak." I rolled my eyes. She had some nerve after she'd just finished talking about hot caramel a minute ago.

"Yes, the Lord spoke to me, and he told me that it was time to get real. I don't know who this is for today, but whoever you are out there, the Lord has got a word for you today. It's time to get real, and so I'll be the one to start off with the realness."

Granny and I looked at each other. I'd never seen the pastor do this before. I knew that I hadn't been here in quite some time, but Granny looked just as surprised as I was. Pastor Richards had always been a great preacher, but I had a feeling he was about to take it to another level.

As Pastor Richards sat there, he began to talk. "See, you didn't even want to come to church today." I felt a slight twinge of guilt when he said that, because I knew I hadn't even wanted to get out of the bed this morning. "You laid in that bed, and you thought of every excuse you could come up with on why not to come. And it wasn't because you were lazy or that you had something better to do. Let me tell you why you laid in that bed." Feeling an energy in the room, I leaned forward in anticipation. I really wanted to hear what he was going to say. "Last night, you went through hell." His voiced boomed throughout the sanctuary, and there were shouts and amens from the all around the room. "Last night something rocked your world." I squirmed uncomfortably in my seat. *Is he talking to me?*

chapter 5

"You have gone through life, and you have had problems, and God has brought you through. But last night wasn't just a little *annoying* problem. Last night was different. It was different because your heart was broken. It was broken into a million little pieces. There was no rationalizing it, and there was no reasoning it. And last night you cried, maybe even screamed because the pain was almost unbearable." *He is talking to me.* I began to feel myself getting emotional. I told myself I had to keep control. But the more he talked, the harder it was. "So you dragged yourself in here today, against your own will. And you're sitting there, dressed up, looking pretty as ever. And you've fooled a lot of people in here. But He sees all and He knows all. He knows that right now, you're dying inside."

I began to cry then. I had never experienced anything like this before. It was as if every word he spoke was being spoken to me. How could he know what I was going through? Was it that obvious? Pastor Richards's voice roared with a spiritual excitement that was contagious as more and more members began to stand. "Yes, He knows your pain. He watched last night as you cried. He waited for you to call His name because all He wanted to do was comfort you. You never called His name, and so you cried yourself to sleep. And when you woke up and realized the nightmare wasn't a dream, you wondered how you'd even gone to sleep in the first place. Well, God gave you that sleep. You had to have it, or else you would have lost your mind up in there."

I felt myself began to shake as his words pierced through me. I was trying so hard to keep control. I was scared of this feeling inside. I felt as though I were battling with something. It had been a while since I'd been to church, but I knew the Lord and I'd been raised in the church. And while I always enjoyed a good sermon, I'd never been one to shout, run, or catch the Holy Ghost. I didn't have anything against it. It had just never happened to me. But today was so different, today I felt something stirring on the inside, as I'd heard Granny say before.

Pastor Richards jumped up and began to walk around the pulpit as he talked. "I came by to tell you that it's time to stop pretending and get real. Stop pretending that you're not sitting there in pain." Suddenly Pastor Richards stopped and looked around as if he were looking for someone in the crowd. The entire church sat in anticipation, and if I leaned forward anymore, I was going to fall on the floor. But I couldn't help myself. Something was propelling me forward. It appeared that Pastor Richards was looking in my direction. I shifted nervously in my seat. Finally his gaze stopped and settled on me. Instantly, I felt exposed. I looked around to see who'd noticed, but no one but the pastor seemed to be looking at me. His powerful voice took on a soothing tone as he talked. "He wants you to know that you are loved. And His thoughts of you are good thoughts. He understands you're in pain, and He is just waiting for you to turn to Him. Only He can heal your wounds."

As Pastor Richards continued to talk, I began to feel as if a weight were being lifted. The events of the last couple of days had shaken and changed my entire world. And this morning, I'd stood in front of the mirror and made sure my appearance was perfect. I hadn't wanted anyone at church to see even a hint of what I was going through. But now I let my tears flow freely as it became less and less important what the people in here would think or say.

The pastor was right. I'd had problems in this life, just like everyone else, and by the grace of God, I'd always made it through. But this, Bryce, had shattered me. Completely. Out of habit, I kept trying to reason. This was ingrained in me by my very profession. I helped people deal with this. Once again, I found there was no reasoning with this, because at moments I really did feel like I was dying inside. I was completely at a loss. I had no idea what to do, where to turn. "He's waiting for you with open arms. Do you know how I know? I know because last night I went through hell. Last night my heart was broken. I had no choice but to call on Him." The entire church seemed to erupt as members jumped out of their seats with shouts encouraging the pastor to go on.

"Tell it pastor."

"Preach it."

"And since we're being real, let me start the realness. Is that all right, Church?" Pastor Richards asked.

"Amen, Pastor," shouted Deaconess Jenkins.

"Make it real, Pastor Richards." I recognized Mrs. Fowler's voice from the back. Pastor Richards, who had just gone back to stand in front of the pulpit, now came back to sit on the edge again as he talked.

"Let me ask you first, was I the only one who had my heart broken?" That single question sent the entire church into a frenzy. Screams and shouts could be heard all across the church. Rain, who up to now had been "amenin" every five seconds, now sat quietly, tears streaming down her face. I struggled and fought for control myself.

As Pastor Richards began to talk about his own private hell and heartbreak, control began to slip more and more out of my grasp. "Well, last night my wife, Carol, and I were eating dinner out on the deck. It was such a beautiful night." He smiled as he remembered. "We sat there laughing and talking about the kids. You all know that Valerie is at Virginia State and Troy is at the University of Florida, so we were talking about taking that second honeymoon we'd always talked about but never seemed to have time for. And then the phone rang. Carol ran inside to answer the phone. After a minute or two I didn't hear anything, so I got up to go inside. We were basically done eating anyway, so I grabbed our plates and headed inside. As I stepped into the house, I heard the most earth-shattering scream I'd ever heard before in my life. Two seconds later, Carol came running around the corner, slamming right into me.

"The plates crashed to the floor, but that was the least of my concerns as my wife of twenty-five years screamed and cried as I'd never seen her scream and cry before. 'Honey, what is it,' I begged her to tell me. But all she would say is, 'Our baby, our baby.' When I noticed that she still had the phone in her hand, I took it from her and was surprised to find our daughter's roommate Crystal on the phone. She was crying herself as she began to tell me what had happened."

Pastor Richards paused for a moment and looked out at the congregation. And for the first time, after years of looking at him up at the pulpit and hearing him preach, I truly saw him. Not as the preacher—it was the husband, the father, the man who was talking to us now. And here he was before us, opening up and baring his soul. And in his face I saw determination and I understood that not only was he determined to confront his own pain, but he was forcing all of us to admit the truth about our own pain and heartbreak. It was time for the masks to come off.

Not a single sound could be heard as Pastor Richards finally continued with his story. "Crystal said that around six in the evening, she'd started to feel sick to her stomach, so she'd told Valerie that she was going to run to the store for a ginger ale. But Valerie, seeing that her friend wasn't feeling well, offered to go in her place. She told Crystal to lie down and rest. She said she'd be back in five minutes. After about fifteen minutes, Crystal got up to look outside. She thought maybe

Valerie had stopped at another friend's dorm room. But Valerie's car wasn't outside, so Crystal called her cell phone, but there was no answer. Crystal said that even though Valerie hadn't really been gone that long, she was starting to feel uneasy. For whatever reason, she decided to walk, not drive, to see what was keeping Valerie. The store was right down the road. So she started walking toward the store, and then she noticed the crowd and smoke. There was smoke everywhere. Crystal said she started running. She didn't even know why, but she felt she had to run. She pressed through the crowd, and that's when she saw it. Valerie's car was in the middle of the road...on fire. The police were there, and when Crystal tried to get to Valerie's car, an officer held her back. Just then there was an explosion, and Crystal screamed. The officer still holding on to Crystal told her that the ambulance had just taken Valerie to the hospital five minutes before.

"Crystal said she rushed back to the dorm to get her car to go to the hospital. And that's where she was calling us from, the hospital. Crystal told me that my baby girl had been on her way back from the store when she was hit head on by a drunk driver. She's in a coma, and in two hours, Carol and I will catch a plane to Virginia to be with our daughter." It was at this point that Pastor Richards, the father, simply broke down. Deacon Brown moved toward the pastor to help, but Pastor Richards waved his hand as if to say he was okay. Some members of the congregation were openly crying now, but most of us just sat there in shock. Pastor Richards stood up then and faced us.

"So, Church, I heard the alarm go off this morning, and I decided that I wasn't coming in today. I made up my mind that I was going to call assistant Pastor Maurice Graysdon to cover the services. I was just hurting too much, and Carol had already said she just couldn't do it. And then the phone rang. It was Clara-Ann, and she said that she'd called just to pray for me." Pastor Richards stopped for a moment to smile at Granny. "Church, you know it's just something about when a seasoned saint gets to praying for you. As soon as she started praying, I began to feel the Holy Spirit move. By the time she finished, I felt peace and strength and just the love of Christ. And I told Carol that I was coming in today.

"When I came in, I was just planning on preaching the sermon that I had prepared all week, but God spoke two words to me: 'Be real.' See, we come here every week. We want to hear a good word, we want to be delivered, but we want it all in a nice little neat package." Pastor Richards began to walk as he talked, and you could just see that spiritual energy again. "Sometimes, saints, you can't have it in a nice little package. Sometimes you've got to go through the pain and it gets messy." His energy was catching. The congregation came alive again as amens and shouts could be heard all over the church.

"It gets messy, Pastor," I heard one of the Roberson twins yell out. Pastor Richards walked over to the pew right in front of mine and sat down. He looked at the members on the pew.

"Do you know that if you actually shared what you are going through, three people on this same pew might be delivered?" He stood up and faced us again. "This is not directed to anyone in particular; it's directed at all of us. We've got to start being real. As Christians, we've got to reach out to each other in love and stop trying to keep up appearances."

"Preach, Pastor Richards, preach," I heard a voice from a few pews over say.

"I'll leave that for another sermon on another day." He ran back up to the pulpit. "Church, let me ask you a question: are you ready for a change?" It sounded as if I heard a million voices say, "Yes!"

"You know, Church, they say the race is not given to the swift nor to the strong."

"Amen." Two women in front of me gave each other a high-five, and I heard one say, "Pastor Richards is on fire today." And she was right. He was filled with the spirit, and it was spilling onto the congregation.

"Speak, Pastor, speak," someone behind me yelled.

Pastor Richards ran down the steps from the pulpit and stood in front of the church as he faced us once again. "Now, I know that not everyone is going to get what I'm about to do. First of all, it's not traditional. It's out of the box, out of the norm. And I'm sure some of you will say I'm just plain crazy. But sometimes, drastic life changes call for drastic measures. For those of us that are too cute or have too much pride to be this real, this isn't for you. This is for those people who had their heart broken last night. Or maybe it wasn't last night. Maybe it was two days ago, a week, a month, or even a year ago. Whenever it was, it still hurts, and I know you're tired of the pain." He looked around the congregation, and once again I felt as if he were looking at me.

"I know you're out there. And you're still in shock. You don't know whether you're comin' or goin.' But my Father knows what you need, and He says He'll be with you, but you've got to stay in the race." Pastor Richards seemed to begin to position himself into a running stance. *What is he about to do?* "I know that whoever is tired of the pain, tired of feeling brokenhearted, will follow my actions. This calls for truth and realness, and those who take advantage of this moment will be delivered. And those who refuse to even admit, much less let go of the pain, will stay trapped in the same nightmare that will only keep replaying itself over and over. So here we go. Those who are with me, let go and let God and realize that no matter what happens, we've got to stay in the race. Let's go!" And with that, Pastor Anthony Richards broke out into a sprint down the middle aisle.

For a moment, no one said anything, but then the church went wild with shouts of praise to the Lord. I watched as Pastor Richards ran, his arms and legs pumping in sheer determination. He burst through the doors. Sunlight poured into the church, and we all heard Pastor Richards as he yelled at the top of his lungs, "I'm still in the race." The entire church was on its feet now. I had no choice but to stand there shaking as the Holy Spirit began to move through me. I cried out in the sheer wonderment of it all, "Thank you, Jesus."

People began to line up in the front of the church, while others shouted, ran, and danced in the Holy Spirit. I could hear the prayers of the elders as they lifted up their voices and hands to praise the Lord. Granny moved closer to me, to comfort me I thought. "Excuse me, baby. I need to get by." I moved aside to let her by. I watched as she walked to the front of the line and asked the young lady standing there, "Can I please go first?" The young lady hugged Granny.

"Yes, you most certainly can, Clara-Ann." Granny positioned herself the same way she'd seen Pastor Richards, and while the stance wasn't exactly the same, you could tell she was getting ready for something. Smiling, Granny looked at me then and said, "This is for you, Leah baby." And then she began to run. I stood there in utter amazement as I watched her. She wasn't really sprinting. It was more half run, half shuffle, but it was the most powerful thing I'd ever seen. Tears of pure wonderment blurred my vision, but I was still able to watch as my grandmother reached the doors to the church. She didn't quite burst through like Pastor Richards had, but my Granny made it outside, and everyone one could hear as she yelled, "I'm still in the race."

I felt myself move then, and I walked to join the others in line. One person at a time the race began, as one person would run and the next person in line would step up and wait until the person running would burst through the church doors and shout at the top of their lungs, "I'm still in the race." Something was happening here; I could feel it. And it was unlike anything

I'd ever experienced in any church before. A young man in front of me broke out into a fast sprint and then burst through the doors. Pastor Richards, who up to now had remained outside, stepped into the doorway of the church.

"I don't care if the doors are knocked off the hinges. All those who are joining us in this Holy Ghost party, I want you to run through these doors as if your life depended on it. And everyone may not be able to run. If you have to walk, then walk. If you need help walking, grab someone to help you. And if you're in a wheelchair, we'll get someone to push you. Just get here, Church, any way you can. Come and join us in this Holy Ghost praise party."

As he closed the doors again, I stepped up. I was next in line to join in the race. I stood there for a moment as I mentally let go of everything. This wasn't about my profession or what people might say. I let go of pride, nervousness, and fear. Looking around at the faces surrounding me, I could see people cheering me on. Others stood there, so filled with the Spirit all they could do was stand there with tears streaming downing their face. They were letting go too. But it was Granny who truly inspired me. I was in awe of her selfless act of love. She had done this for me, and now I had to do this for myself.

Then I began to run. *"Your heart was broken last night."* Pastor Richards's words rang in my ears as I ran past the pews. From the pulpit to the doors of the church was really only about a ten-second run, but even though I was running as fast as I could, I felt as if I were in slow motion. And that was just fine with me, because I'd never felt this free in my entire life. Once again, the events of the past few days flashed through my mind. *Lord, please help me through this. I need you.* Bryce's hurtful words and actions pierced through me once again, but still I continued to run as the tears stung my face. I was no longer aware of anything except my run and my own private conversation with God. It was as if it were just Him and me in this thing together. *Jesus, I can't make it through this without you.*

Through the pain and the tears that were still stinging my face, I instantly felt peace. Immediately, I was engulfed in His comfort. Sunlight bathed my face, and I lifted my face toward heaven as I shouted, "I'm still in the race." Dropping to my knees on the front yard of the church, I prayed. *Thank You, Lord, for this peace. Thank You for Your love. I rededicate my life to You Father. Thank You, Jesus, thank You.* After praying, I sat up and that's when I noticed all the people. There were members of the congregation everywhere. I hadn't realized how many people had run this race.

As I stood up, Rain ran over to hug me, and I hugged her back. There was something different about her now. She seemed real. "Rain, if you ever need to talk to me, I am here," I told her.

"As my psychologist?" She looked away for a moment and then faced me again. "I guess I could use one." I looked her into her eyes.

"As a friend, Rain." Her smile was bright as it lit up her entire face.

"Thank you, Leah. I could really use a friend right now." We exchanged numbers and hugged again before Rain left to find Pastor Richards. She said she wanted him to pray with her. I looked around the yard until I spotted Granny. She was praying with three young ladies. I walked over, but I stood at a distance until they were done praying. Once they were done, the young ladies left. I walked over to Granny, and we hugged for a long time. "Thank you for doing what you did for me. And thank you for bringing us here today."

"It wasn't me that brought you here today. It was God." We both looked around at all the people who were smiling and praying and talking. This was true fellowship here today. Pastor Richards walked over to join us.

"Leah, I am so glad you made it today. I've missed seeing you and your family around the church. Believe me, Clara-Ann always gives us updates on the children, but we've just missed you."

"Well, Pastor Richards, I am so glad that I came today. I know I haven't been here in a while, but it was as if I was truly meant to be here today. Thank you."

"Please don't thank me. Our Father had this today. I said it before, but I'll tell you again, I wasn't coming in myself today. But when God moves, you have no choice but to follow. He had this young lady here call and pray." Pastor Richards hugged Granny, and she laughed as she hugged him back.

"Pastor, I am sorry to hear about Valerie. How are you holding up?" I asked.

"I am holding up just fine now. You know, today wasn't planned. It just happened." Granny placed a hand on Pastor Richard's shoulder.

"No, Pastor, this was Jesus. He was in this place today."

"You're right about that, Clara-Ann," said Pastor Richards. He smiled at both of us as he talked. "You know, some of the best miracles come out of brokenness. Last night I was broken, but today, today was a good day. And I feel whole again. Valerie is still in a coma, but I'm going to trust and have faith in my Jesus that we're going to make it through this. I am getting on that plane with hope."

"Now let me ask you, Leah, are you okay?"

"Yes, Pastor, I am much better now."

"Okay, I am glad to hear that. Leah, I can see you're in the middle of a storm. I don't know the details like He does, but I saw the hurt and the pain in your eyes today. Your heart was broken, wasn't it?"

I looked at him and answered truthfully. After today, there was no more pretending, no more hiding. "Yes, Pastor, my heart is broken. And that's how I know I was supposed to be here today."

"Well, my sister in Christ, I want you to know today is a new beginning for your life. Now, because you're in the middle of a storm, you're going to have to trust in Him, because there are still some hard days ahead. What you experienced today was God's love and peace. But when you leave this church today, that doesn't mean that you're not going to cry sometimes. Just remember that He loves you and He will never leave you."

"Thank you, I needed to hear that, Pastor," I said as I hugged him. "Everything that happened today, I needed it. It wasn't traditional, but it was truly needed."

"Yes, my sisters in Christ, we all needed this today. God is an awesome God. He always knows just what we need, even when we don't, remember that. Now, ladies, I've got a plane to catch. Let's join everyone else so we can close in prayer." We joined the rest of the congregation as Pastor Richards called out, "Everyone, if we can please gather around and join hands, we're going to close in prayer. After prayer, there is no rush. You can stay as long as you'd like to fellowship. Pastor Graysdon will lock up this evening because, as you know, I have a flight to Virginia this afternoon." We all joined hands. I marveled at all the people stretched across the churchyard. We stood here together, not judging each other, but we stood together in love, every hand clasped together in the comfort of Christ. Once Pastor Richards saw that we were all together, he began to pray. "Please let us all bow our heads. Heavenly Father, we come to you today, and we just want to say thank You, Lord. Thank You for just being You. You are so mighty and wonderful. Jesus, we need a special touch from You today as we leave this place. We came to You today broken and in need, and You have restored us. Thank You, Jesus. Thank You, Father. Thank You for Your love, thank You for Your mercy, and thank You for Your grace, Father."

"Yes, Lord," said Granny as she squeezed my hand.

"Lord, no matter what happens, please help us to remember that You are with us. No matter how dark the night may be, let us remember that Your light will shine in the morning."

"Yes, Lord," I heard voices all around me say.

"If we can just make it through the night, Lord, it will be all right. Give us strength to stay in the race, Jesus. We thank You, we love You, and we bless Your holy name. And the church said..."

"Amen," we all echoed.

"Now, Church, keep our family in your prayers as we travel. When you all leave here today, and even throughout the week, read and study Hebrews chapter twelve, verses one through three. Maybe I already said it, but I'll say it again in case anyone missed it: everything in life doesn't change overnight. God is all-powerful and yes, He can fix any and everything in the blink of an eye. But there are lessons to be learned. Your strength and your faith will grow, and through these trials you will become closer to God than you've ever been in your entire life. And in your darkest moments, He will be there, helping you along the way. Stay in the race. Always remember that He loves you. I love you, and I'm praying that you all have a blessed week."

Pastor Richards shook hands with members as he prepared to leave. The crowd broke up as people went to their cars to leave. Granny and I headed back toward the church to get the kids. She gently touched my arm, and I knew what she was going to ask before she spoke. "What happened, Leah?" I was soaring high right now and didn't want to go into any of the gory details right now, so I put on a smile and did my best to reassure Granny. "Bryce and I had an argument, but I am fine.

I don't want you to worry." She smiled that knowing smile, and I knew she knew there was more, but she wasn't going to push. "Inside the church, while I was sitting there, I could feel your pain. That's what caused me to move. I don't know what it is, but know that I am here for you."

"Thank you, and I love you."

"I love you too." We continued on to the church, but we didn't even make it to the door before the kids came running out.

They ran up to us, both of them talking a mile a minute. "Mama, can we come back Wednesday night. They're having a youth program. Plus, my friend Tim goes here." I watched my son as he talked excitedly about his experience today.

"Yes, we can come back Wednesday night."

"Mommy, I had fun too." Malaysia, who was not willing to be left out, began to tell us about all the fun she'd had in children's church. I was glad they'd had a good time and learned something about the Lord at the same time. After today, I couldn't imagine staying away. God was truly in this place.

I dropped Granny off with a promise to pick her up for Wednesday night Bible study. As I drove away, She stood at her front door, still waving. We'd shared something truly miraculous, and I would never forget this day. It truly felt like the first day of the rest of my life. I still didn't have any answers. Who knew what was going to happen between Bryce and me? All I knew was that I genuinely felt happy. With all the hell that was going on in my life, I knew it was nobody but God that was getting me through this.

We pulled into the driveway, and the first thing I saw was Bryce's car. My heart dropped.

"Daddy's home." Malaysia was so excited she practically hopped out of the car before I completely stopped. I didn't have a chance to say anything to her as she took off running toward the house. Panicking, I sat there for a moment. I wasn't ready for this. I looked over at Darren, who was looking at me. He was trying to judge my reaction. I attempted a smile, but I could tell Darren wasn't buying it. *Teenagers are too smart these days,* I thought as we both got out of the car. The truth was, I didn't know what to feel. There were a million emotions all jumbled up inside. I'd just come from this miraculous experience at church, and now I was being thrust back into my harsh reality. But Pastor Richards's words rang in my ears: *"Everything in life doesn't change overnight."* I took a deep breath and walked into the house.

chapter 6

When I walked in the door, I saw that Malaysia was still hugging her father. Darren spoke to Bryce but continued on to his room. "Darren, before you go to your room, please do me a favor and order a couple of pizzas." I usually cooked my Sunday dinner on Saturday nights, but I hadn't taken anything out yesterday, and at this point I just didn't feel like cooking now.

"Okay, Ma." Darren's whole body was tense as he spoke to me. I made a mental note to talk to him later. It wasn't that he'd been rude, but he was already showing hostility toward Bryce, and he didn't even know what was going on yet. Or did he?

"Hello, Bryce," I managed to get out. Malaysia was standing with him, so for now she was my safety net.

"Malaysia, baby, let me speak to Mommy for a few minutes, okay?" So much for the safety net.

"But, Daddy, I haven't seen you in days. You're not going anywhere else, are you, Daddy?" It broke my heart to hear the desperation in my child's voice. I kneeled down in front of her until we were eye level.

"Honey, Daddy and I are just going to talk. Right now, no one is going anywhere. We promise we will come and get you and let you know what's going on. Okay?"

"Okay," Malaysia said shakily as she walked away.

I walked into the kitchen with the pretense of getting something to drink, even though I wasn't hungry or thirsty at all. Bryce followed me into the kitchen and sat at one of the barstools. Getting some juice from the refrigerator, I took a seat at the kitchen table. Bryce turned around on the barstool and faced me. For a moment we just sat there in silence. "Leah, I really don't know where to start. I know that I've messed up. I am so sorry for all of this."

"Tell me, Bryce, are you sorry for sleeping with her or for going into business with her? Which one?" Sighing, Bryce moved from the bar stool to join me at the table. We sat across from each other. Bryce stared at me, trying to read me. I'd told myself I'd be civilized, but as I sat there looking at the man I'd given the last ten years of my life to, I became angrier by the moment.

"Leah, I ended things with her today."

"Oh, like you told me you ended things with her last time? Bryce, you destroyed the trust I had in you. Do you really think I'll believe anything you have to say?"

"Okay, I guess I deserve that, but I'm telling you I broke it off. I realized that I want to be with my family. Please tell me I have a chance." Bryce reached for my hand, which only angered me even more. Snatching my hand back, I stared at him in disbelief. I couldn't believe he would even have the audacity to try and touch me after all of this. Jumping up from the table, Bryce paced around the kitchen. "Oh, so now I can't even touch my own wife? Look, Leah, we've got to move beyond this, because we're going to make this marriage work one way or another."

"And what the hell is that supposed to mean, Bryce? Do you really think you have any right to come in here demanding anything from me?"

"You have been sleeping with a married woman for three years now.

Don't try to turn this thing all around on me. You are at fault here too." Before I knew it, I was in his face.

"Are you serious?" I felt my voice rising, but I couldn't help myself. This fool was crazy. "And tell me, how is it my fault that you went out and slept with another woman? And not once, but for *three years*! And not only that, you have a business with her." I was screaming now. I turned away from him, because looking at his face disgusted me. And the things that I was thinking about doing to him in this kitchen weren't godly at all. I had to calm down for myself and for the sake of the children. I didn't want them to see us like this. Bryce walked over and stood in front of me, so once again we were facing each other.

"I'm really not in business with her. I just helped with the financial part of it." I could only stare at him. He actually thought he was making things better with what he was saying. "Look, all I'm trying to say is that our marriage has had issues for a long time now. It's not just about the affair, Leah." I stared at him in disbelief. He just refused to take responsibility for what he'd done.

"Yes, you are absolutely right. We *have* had problems for years. But maybe if you would've kept it in your pants long enough, we could've worked on our issues. Did you ever think about that, Bryce?" Bryce was saved from having to answer as Darren burst into the kitchen.

"Ma, the pizza man is here." Darren took one look at us and frowned. "Ma, are you okay?" There was my little protector again. I walked over and put my arm around him.

"I'm just fine, Darren. Now let's go get that pizza."

I led my son out of the kitchen, glad to get away from Bryce, even if it was just for a moment. I paid for the pizza and handed it to Darren. "Why don't you take this to the movie room and pop in that new DVD I bought the other day, and I'll bring both of you something to drink." Right now I was very glad for the built in movie theatre the previous owner had had installed. It would keep the kids distracted, and the room was all the way on the other side of the house.

"Ma, are you sure you're going to be okay?" I hadn't fooled my son at all.

"Darren, yes, I am fine. Daddy and I are just talking."

"It sounded more like yelling to me," Darren said.

"I'm sorry about that. Sometimes when people are having a disagreement, you're both trying to get your point across and sometimes voices rise. I'm sorry you heard that. I am going back to talk to Bryce, and I want you to go ahead to the movie room. We all will be just fine, okay?"

"Okay." Darren was reluctant to leave. I hugged him and kissed him lightly on the forehead. "Thank you for taking such good care of your mother. I really am okay, so stop worrying. Go ahead and watch the movie. I know you've been wanting to see it." Finally assured that I was okay, Darren took the pizzas and headed to the movie room. I breathed a sigh of relief. The last thing I needed was for Darren to go overboard trying to protect me. I could see it now. He'd confront Bryce on my behalf, and then all hell would break loose. No, we weren't having any of that today.

After getting the kids drinks and making sure they were settled, I went back into the kitchen and sat down. "Okay, Leah, I guess I deserve your anger. I am sorry. I just want to make things right." He walked toward me and attempted to hug me or hold me. Whichever one, I wanted no part of it. I backed away from him.

"Please, Bryce, don't touch me. I seriously cannot handle that right now." He stopped right in front of me, and we stood there facing each other. He actually looked hurt by the fact that I didn't want him to touch me.

"So what is it that you want, Leah? Do you just want to get a divorce? I think we should at least try to make this work. But what do you want?" I didn't know what I wanted. On one hand, I wanted to scream at him to get out and never come back. *How can I ever trust him again? Is it really over between us? I can't stand for him to touch me right now. Will I ever let him touch me again?* All these questions swirled around in my head. And then I heard a phone ringing. A few seconds later, Malaysia came into the kitchen. "Mommy, it's your cell phone." She handed me the phone and was gone again. Looking at the caller ID, I saw that it was Taylor Roberts. I'd given her my cell number before, but she'd never called. I wondered what was going on. "Hello, Taylor, this is Dr. Leah. How are you?"

"Dr. Leah, you've got to come," Taylor said breathlessly. Now concerned by the sound of her voice, I turned to Bryce and signaled to him to give me a minute. I walked into the living room and sat down.

"Taylor, what is going on?"

"She's gone crazy. She's throwing all my clothes outside." In the background, I could hear someone yelling. "I called Uncle Graye, but there was no answer. Please, Dr. Leah, you've got to come. I don't have anyone else."

"Okay, Taylor, calm down. I'll be there in about ten minutes. Stay calm, and do not argue back if your Aunt Louise starts yelling again. Wait for me. I'll be there as soon as I can."

I hung up with Taylor, and as I stood up, I saw that Bryce had come to the living room. "Leah, I heard you talking to your patient. I can stay with the children. Please let me at least do that. If you want me to leave when you get back, I will. But I can do this for you. Let me, please." All of a sudden he was being so understanding, but I knew he was going to try to do anything to get back into my good graces. I wasn't sure of a lot right now, but I knew he loved our children and he'd never do anything to harm them.

"Okay, Bryce. I really appreciate it. It sounds like there is an emergency with my patient. They live about ten minutes away, so I won't be long. I'll go tell the kids now. Thank you again." I left him in the living room as I headed to the movie room to tell the kids that they'd be here with Daddy for a little while. I knew Malaysia wouldn't mind. It was Darren that I was worried about.

Ten minutes later, I was on my way to Louise Roberts's home. I had sensed that all was not well with Taylor and her aunt in our last session, but Taylor had been so excited that I'd decided to wait before I approached the subject of her and her aunt. Taylor had been the happiest I'd ever seen her, so I'd let her bask in that happiness before we moved on. Maybe I should have forced the issue. Now I just hoped Taylor was okay. Finally, after what seemed like forever, I arrived at the Roberts's residence. I noticed two cars parked there. I recognized the beige Lexus as Louise Roberts's car, but I didn't recognize the white Hummer. I didn't know too much about cars, but it was really nice. It actually looked brand new, like it had just been driven off the parking lot of a dealership. Taylor came running out of the house when she saw me pull into the driveway. She hopped into the car with me. "Dr. Leah, thank you for coming. I am so glad you're here. Uncle Graye is here too now. He's inside talking to Aunt Louise. Do you want to go inside?"

Turning to look at Taylor, I saw that she was better than when I'd initially talked to her on the phone. "You seem better than when I talked to you a few minutes ago, but are you really okay?" I was concerned for her. She'd made such good progress lately, and I didn't want her to have a setback. For the first time, she'd shown some real confidence, and I wanted to build on that.

"I am okay now. Uncle Graye is here. When I couldn't reach him, I freaked out and called you. I'm sorry about this." Then she smiled sheepishly. "But I'm still glad you're here."

"Taylor, you know I'm always here for you, but what happened? What led to all of this?" As quickly as the smile had come, it was gone.

"My father called from prison tonight. Aunt Louise answered the phone. Normally, she talks to him and then after they hang up, she tells me that he asked about me and that he loves me. But tonight she talked to him for a few minutes, and then she said he wanted to speak to me. Well, I told her I didn't want to talk to him. We started arguing because she tried to make me get on the phone with him." Taylor looked away then, and I could tell she was trying not to cry.

"Dr. Leah, I really wasn't trying to be disrespectful to my aunt. I am just not ready to talk to him. And I couldn't get her to understand that. She hung up with my father and started screaming at me. She said that I had to forgive him and she said that I was going to have to start going to see him. When I told her I didn't want to see him, she went ballistic and started yelling about how I was going to follow her rules or get out. When I wouldn't agree to go see him this weekend, she grabbed some of my things and threw them out of the house. She said I had to get out and that she wasn't going to have someone disrespecting her in her own house. That's when I called you. But right after I called you,

Uncle Graye showed up. He told me to go to my room while he talked to her. I didn't hear everything, but I did hear Uncle Graye tell Aunt Louise that I am coming to live with him, starting tonight." Now that was something Taylor wasn't upset about at all. I could tell by the way her voice changed on that last statement. "I mean, I don't want Aunt Louise to be upset with me. I just think she's trying to force me into doing something I'm not ready for. I don't know if I'll ever be ready to see him. Every time I think of him, I think of what he did to my mother." She was silent for a moment. "It's probably for the best that I go live with Uncle Graye." Hearing a sound coming from the house, we both turned and looked as the front door opened.

My mouth dropped open as the mystery man with the beautiful gray eyes from church stepped outside in plain view. "Dr. Leah, are you okay?" Taylor was laughing now as she watched me.

"Um … yes. Is that your Uncle Graye?"

"Yes, it is. Come on. Let's go so I can introduce you to him." Taylor got out of the car and ran toward her uncle. I sat there for a moment as I grasped the concept. Why hadn't I put two and two together the first time I'd looked into his gray eyes? *Because you were too busy thinking about hot caramel.* Stop it, I told myself. This was no time to be having these kinds of thoughts. I got out of the car and started toward them. Just then, my cell phone rang. It was Bryce.

"Hello, Bryce, what's up? How are the kids?" I asked him.

"That's why I'm calling. I went to check on them in the movie room, and they were both knocked out asleep. I got them both into bed. I just wanted to let you know that everything at home is okay." *No, everything at home is not okay,* I thought. But this wasn't the time or the place.

"Okay, well thank you for calling to let me know that the kids are okay. I shouldn't be too much longer, so I'll talk to you when I get home."

"Okay then. Leah?"

"What is it Bryce?"

"I love you." Not knowing how to respond to that I just hung up. I approached Taylor and her uncle, and I saw the recognition in his eyes. He remembered me too.

"Dr. Leah, this is my uncle Graye. Uncle Graye, this is Dr. Leah. Well, Dr. Gordon actually. She lets me call her Dr. Leah." We both laughed as Taylor talked excitedly.

"It's nice to meet you, Mr. Barrington," I said, extending my hand to him. As we shook hands, I felt a tiny jolt of electricity, which was unusual because in ten years of marriage, I'd shaken hands with men before. *This is so different,* I thought. And it was different, because I'd never felt anything like this before. It was that same connection that I'd felt the first time I'd seen him. I couldn't explain it. It felt deeper than a physical attraction, but what else could it be? I didn't even know him.

"Please call me Graye. And let me say, that's a really nice car you have there." I turned and looked at my car, a baby blue Mercedes. It was brand spanking new. It had been my birthday gift to myself a month ago. You only turn thirty once, I'd told myself as I drove it from the dealership. I turned back to Graye and smiled.

"God is good, isn't He?"

"Yes, He is, all the time," he said, returning the smile. "Taylor, go ahead inside and talk to your aunt Louise. She just wants to apologize to you, okay?" Taylor looked reluctant to leave us.

"Okay, Uncle Graye. But, Dr. Leah, don't leave before you say good-bye."

"You know I wouldn't do that," I said, playfully pulling on her ponytail. She smiled at both of us as she walked into the house.

Louise had one of those old-fashioned porches that I loved. It reminded me of Granny's home. It even had one of those old swings I'd loved as a child; I couldn't resist sitting on it. Graye sat diagonal to me in one of the chairs Louise had on her porch. "So how did you do it, Graye? When Taylor called, she was hysterical and I could hear Louise yelling in the background. So what's your secret?"

"Prayer." I laughed when he said that. He smiled too, but I saw that he was serious. "Leah—oh, can I call you Leah?"

"Of course."

"Well, Leah, I got Taylor's message, and on the way over here I had to do some serious praying. See, from the moment Taylor was born, that little girl just wrapped herself around my heart, and she hasn't let go since. And just the thought of her being mistreated drove me crazy. So I wasn't joking when I said I had to pray for strength to approach this situation in the right way. I needed God to step in, fast and in a hurry."

I studied Graye for a moment. I couldn't help but be impressed by this man. He'd lost so much, and here he was still praying and asking God for help. I'd seen a lot of people turn away from God when tragedy struck. I couldn't even say for sure what I would do in the same situation. And here he was being the voice of reason when I knew it had to be hard for him even dealing with the sister of the man who'd murdered his twin sister.

"So what's going to happen now?" I asked him.

"We talked and decided it would be best for Taylor to come and live with me. I am going to go to court and get legal custody. Louise thinks it's a good idea, and she's not going to fight me on it or anything. I'm sorry this happened tonight, but I am excited about Taylor coming to live with me."

"And so is Taylor."

"Yes, she is." Just when I thought he couldn't be any more gorgeous, his smile lit up his face, and those beautiful gray eyes just glowed. They drew me in and held me captive. Sitting there listening to the plans he was making for himself and Taylor, I took a moment to study this man who intrigued me. At church I'd seen him from a distance, but now, sitting here, he looked almost bigger than life, like he'd literally just stepped out of the pages of a magazine. And what was even more attractive was the fact that he seemed totally unaware of his effect.

He was tall—I'd say at least six foot four—and he was very well built. He had a low haircut, just the way I liked. I don't know what it was, but there was just something about a fresh cut. And Rain was right about one thing. His skin really did make me think of caramel. He was almost what people called a "pretty boy." But there was a strength and manliness about him as well.

I watched his mouth as he laughed about something Taylor had said to him. He had to have the most beautiful lips I'd ever seen. *Girl, get ahold of yourself.* "Leah, calling Leah."

"Oh, I'm sorry, Graye. What did you say?"

"I asked if you wanted something to drink."

I had to get out of here before I embarrassed myself anymore than I already had. Here he was asking me a simple question, and I was daydreaming about him. "No thank you," I said, standing up. "I guess it's about time for me to go. Can you please get Taylor so I can tell her good night?"

"Sure, let me get her." Graye went in search of Taylor while I waited on the porch. I had no idea what was going on with me, but I had to get out of here quick, fast, and in a hurry. This attraction was new to me, and it was making me very nervous. *Okay, think rationally,* I told myself. Yes, I felt something when I looked at him, but this had to be because of everything I was going through with Bryce. It was also the way he looked at me, as if he really *saw* me. I couldn't remember the last time Bryce and I had actually looked at each other and really *saw* each other. Regardless of this attraction, I was still a married woman, and fantasizing about some man was the last thing I needed to be doing. Besides that, he was my patient's uncle, and I didn't even want to begin to think of the legalities of that.

A few minutes later, Graye returned with Taylor. "Well, young lady, I am getting ready to leave. I just wanted to tell you goodnight."

"Thank you again, Dr. Leah, for coming. You're always there for me." Taylor hugged me. She was such a sweet girl.

"You don't need to thank me. You know I'm always here for you. Now don't forget we have a session next week, but if you need me before then just call."

"I will, and drive safely." Taylor then turned to her uncle. "Uncle Graye, I'm going to get a few more of my things before we go." And then she was gone again. She was still so excited about the move. I could hear it in her voice. She would be just fine with this turn of events.

"Well, Graye, it doesn't look like my presence was really needed tonight, but it was nice meeting you anyway. Have a good night," I said, shaking his hand again.

"Before you go, I just want to tell you thank you for coming tonight. I know that you're her psychologist, but you didn't have to come here tonight, so thank you for caring." Out of all the patients that I'd had over the years, Taylor had been the one to worm her way into my heart. Without even trying, over time, she'd just become more than a patient to me. I remembered her first office visit like it was yesterday. She looked so young and scared. But it was the eyes that really touched me. There was so much sadness when she looked at me. That first session we hadn't really talked at all, and I'd watched as she familiarized herself with the office. At one point she'd stared long and hard at the pictures I had of Darren and Malaysia. When the session was over, right before she'd walked out, she turned and gave me the saddest smile I'd ever seen. I had vowed to myself right then to do whatever it took to help her.

"You don't have to thank me, Graye. I really care about that little girl in there. I told her that I'll always be here for her, and I will. But now that she has her Uncle Graye back, she may not need me anymore," I said, laughing.

"Hey, she talks about you to me just as much as she talks about me to you, I'm sure. So we're even. She needs both of us, doctor."

"Good night, Graye."

"Good night, Leah."

chapter 7

On the way home, I thought of my conversation with Graye. Besides the fact that he was beyond good looking, he was very easy to talk to. It was also clear that he really loved his niece, and the fact that he was a man of God was an even bigger plus. *Wait a minute, what am I doing?* Mentally giving myself a shake, I realized exactly what I had been doing: sizing Graye Barrington up, something I had no business doing. Instantly, I felt guilty. No matter what, I was still a married woman. Who knew what was going to happen with Bryce and me, but having fantasies about another man wasn't going to help at all. *Lord, please forgive me.*

Determined to block Graye out of my mind, I popped in a new gospel CD. I had to seriously get my mind right. As the sounds of Kirk Franklin's *Hero* filled the air, my mind went back to earlier today to the church service. I had to look at today as a new beginning, despite everything I was going through right now. I didn't have to rush and make any rash decisions. No, I would take this week to just pray and really think about everything before I made any decisions at all. As

I drove, I sang along with the music. By the time I turned onto my street, I was at peace again.

Before I could even get my key in the door, Bryce opened the door to let me in. Stepping aside to let me by, Bryce closed and locked the door. "So how is your patient?"

"She's had a lot of changes in her young life, but I think she's going to be just fine."

"That's good. Someone named Rain called. She said she's from church. I took her number for you."

"Okay, thanks. I'll call her back in a minute. Are the kids still asleep?" I asked him as I walked to the kitchen. I'd rushed out so quickly earlier, I hadn't even grabbed a slice of pizza. I was going to do some damage to it now. Bryce followed me into the kitchen, delivering the blow. "Um, Leah, the kids demolished the pizza." Groaning, I turned around to face him.

"There's not even one slice left?" I couldn't believe them. How could they have eaten two pizzas?

"Well, Darren and I sort of had a contest going." Bryce laughed, and I laughed with him. It had been a while since we'd laughed together at all, and for a moment, I forgot about our troubles as I pictured Bryce and Darren challenging each other to a pizza duel.

"Now, wait a minute. How much pizza did he eat? I don't want him getting sick, Bryce."

"It's okay. Calm down. I watched him. If anything, it will be me with the stomachache," he said, patting his stomach.

"Well, let me get you something." I started searching for something for a stomachache, and then I stopped.

For the last few minutes, everything had seemed so normal—friendly conversation, even laughter. Even now, I was searching the cabinets for something to make my husband feel better. These were all normal things that go on within a family. But now the hurt and the pain came rushing back full force. I gripped the side of the kitchen counter as I fought for control. I was not going to give him the satisfaction of seeing me break down again. We both stood there for a moment in an uncomfortable silence. Bryce, breaking the silence, cleared his throat. "Um, the pizza is gone, but I just ordered you some food from that new Japanese steakhouse. It should be here soon. Um, okay, so I'll go wait for the delivery guy." Bryce left to go wait in the living room.

Maybe my appetite will return by the time the delivery guy gets here.

By the time the delivery guy had gotten there, I was starving again. Bryce had just sat there and watched the entire time while I ate. Oh, he'd pretended to be doing something, but every time I looked up he was watching me. I'd done my best to ignore him as I tried to enjoy my food. Now here I was in the library. I'd closed the door purposely when I came in here. I was hoping he got the message. Remembering that Rain had called me, I went to the phone to call her. Getting her voicemail, I left her a brief message and hung up. I then settled down with a good book on the couch, but it wasn't long before I heard a soft knock at the library door.

Normally Bryce would have just barged in, but I guessed he was really trying not to set me off. "Leah, it's your mother on the phone." Sighing, I got up to get the phone. I opened the door and took the phone from Bryce. Then I closed the door again, but I hadn't missed the pleading look in his eyes. I honestly didn't know what he expected from me. I was basically still in shock trying to absorb everything that had happened. And I just didn't have any answers for him right now. Turning my attention to the phone, I sat down on the couch again.

"Hey, Mama, how are you?"

"I'm fine. How are you? I haven't heard from you in a couple of days." I had been avoiding her, and with good reason. If there was one other person who knew me it was my mother, Cynthia Foster. Like my grandmother, my mother was one of the strongest black women I knew. If she would have had any inkling of what was going on, she would have been over here ready to go off on Bryce.

"I'm fine. Mama. I've just been a little busy. How is the new deck coming along?" Five years ago, Bryce and I had bought my mother a new home, and recently she'd started this new project of expanding her deck. She was excited about it, and I knew if I got her talking about that, it would take the focus off me. For the next fifteen minutes, she talked of nothing but her new deck. I listened to the sound of her voice. She was happy. I'd been all too happy when we'd surprised her with the house. Success meant nothing if you didn't share it.

We'd also tried to buy a new home for Granny, but she wasn't having it. She'd lived in her home for over thirty years, and she wasn't going anywhere. "I talked to Mama today. She told me what happened at church. I wish I'd been there with y'all." I smiled as I thought of my experience there today.

"I wish you would have been there too. Words can't really describe it. All I can say is God was in that place today."

"Well, I will be at Bible study Wednesday. Are you going?"

"Yes, and the kids had such a good time too, they can't wait to go back. They had friends that were there, and you know the children's ministry always finds new and exciting ways to teach children about God."

"Well, it sounds like the adults also learned something, a new and exciting way to praise God."

"That we did, Mama. That we did."

When I hung up with my mother a few minutes later, I settled down on the couch again to read. Another knock on the door interrupted me before I had read two pages. *Oh forget it, it just wasn't meant to be*, I thought to myself as I got up again to go to the door. "What can I help you with Bryce?" I asked

"I just wanted to see if you wanted to talk?" *Is he serious?*

Looking into his eyes, I could see that he was. I'd spent years begging him to talk to me, to no avail. And now after all of this, he wanted to talk. This was all too much. I felt like I was going to explode at any moment. I guess my expression said it all, because he moved on to his next question. "Well, can I at least stay the night? I'll sleep in the guest room." I wanted to scream at him that no, he could not sleep here tonight. And the fact that he was acting like this, timid and soft-spoken, only irritated me even more. It was because it magnified his guilt that much more. But I also didn't like it when he was defensive either. I just couldn't win for losing. I stared back at this stranger. *Where is the husband I used to trust with my life?* As suddenly as the anger had been there, it was gone. Now there was only sadness.

"Bryce, you can stay tonight. Beyond that, I really don't have any answers." He didn't push, and without another word, he turned and walked away. I closed the door again. Curling up on the couch, I turned off the lamp and just lay there. *Lord, please help us*

The next few days passed by in a blur. When we'd had the incident with Simone's patient, Mr. Goodman, we'd had to cancel all the other appointments. They'd all been rescheduled for this week. Monday and Tuesday were so hectic that Simone, Brooke , and I had barely had time for lunch. Now it was Wednesday, and things were just now starting to get back to normal. I looked at my watch. It was 6:00 p.m., and I was sitting in my office waiting for Simone. She was supposed to be going to Bible study tonight. I knew she was done with her final session for the day. She was probably stalling. I'd had to talk her into going with me.

Getting ready to call her office again, I picked up the phone just as she walked into my office. "Girl, I was getting ready to call you again. Are you ready to go?" I asked her as I hung up the phone.

"As ready as I'll ever be." But I noticed that she seemed a bit hesitant.

"Okay, Simone, what's up? Do you still want to go?" Simone sighed as she sat down on the couch.

"A part of me does want to go. That's why I said yes when you asked me on Monday. I mean, when you told me the experience that you had Sunday, it reminded me of years ago when I was involved in the church. Life-changing experiences like that would happen, and all you could do was stand there and let the Holy Spirit take over. I can't remember exactly when I stopped going to church. I think it happened gradually. I'd gotten involved with Chris, and you know he never wanted to go to church. I think he was allergic." We both laughed at that.

"Girl, you are so crazy."

"No, but with all the drama in my relationship with him, and you and I working so hard to get this practice, I just let life steer me away from what I've always known. But when I thought about going with you tonight, I started getting nervous. I haven't been in so long. And you know me; I've done and said a lot of things that aren't pleasing to God."

"Okay, stop right there. We all have said and done things that are not pleasing to God. Now I'll admit, when I first got to church on Sunday, I was feeling a little guilty myself. Like you, I haven't been to church in a long time. But don't you think He knows that? He knows exactly what we've been up to. He knows what we're going to do before we do it. And despite all of that, He still loves us, still wants us. That's one of the most beautiful things about Christ. He's not like people. When we screw up, He doesn't say, 'That's it. I'm done with you.' He stands there with His arms wide open, waiting for us to come to Him. He forgives us and loves us. And you know what I realized the other day? There are so many things that we don't go to Him with. We just make our own decisions and do what we want to do and then expect Him to fix it. And you know what He does? He shows us more love and mercy and grace. There is just none like Him."

I found myself getting emotional, and I looked over at Simone, who looked like she was getting emotional as well. "While I was there this Sunday, I rededicated my life to Christ. And it wasn't because all of a sudden I think all my problems are going to be solved instantly or that I'm now going to be this perfect saved person. But I believe in Him, Simone, and I just know now that walking with Christ is so much better than walking without Him." We were both crying now. I walked over to my friend and hugged her. "Let's go, we have an appointment at Blessed Life Baptist Church." Simone stood up and grabbed her purse.

"Okay, I'm ready. Let's go. Don't we have to pick up the kids?"

"No, my mother picked them up earlier, and we'll meet them all at the church." I followed Simone out and locked the door behind me.

As we began to walk down the hall, Simone stopped and faced me. "Leah?"

"Yes? What's up?" I asked her.

"I just want to say thank you. I really needed that in there."

"You don't have to thank me, Simone. I'm always there for you, just like you're there for me. And you know, we all need real talk from a real friend sometimes."

"Tell it, sista. You know that's the truth." I laughed as Simone gave me a high-five. "And speaking of truth, we really haven't had time this week to talk. What's going on with Bryce?"

"Girl, that conversation is too heavy for the hallway. That's some sit-down stuff right there. I'll tell you what: you follow me home, we'll drop my car off, and then I'll bring you up to speed, okay?"

"Sounds like a deal."

On the way home, I thought about Bryce. He'd hardly been home all week, claiming he had to work late. And when I did see him, all we seemed to do was argue. Bryce's apologetic demeanor didn't last long at all. After Sunday night, he was back to his usual self—egotistical, defensive, and non-responsive when I tried to talk to him. He refused to accept responsibility for his actions. He was still trying to blame me. But he had the wrong sister on that one. I was a psychologist, and I knew all about mind games. I had no problem accepting the fact that our marriage had been in trouble for years. I'd tried numerous times to work on our marriage, but it takes two. He'd never wanted to talk or go to counseling or do anything to meet me halfway. But the bottom line was no matter what we'd been going through, I didn't deserve this ultimate betrayal from him. I'd bent over backward trying to do any and everything to save our marriage, while he never even tried. Instead, he'd run to another woman. Over the years, in the midst of heated arguments and accusations, we'd threatened each other with divorce. But now, for the first time, I seriously considered it. I just didn't know if there was any coming back from this.

Deep in thought, I almost missed my turn. Turning on to my street, I noticed a truck in my driveway. Once I got closer, I could see Bryce's car was parked in front of what looked like a moving truck. *What is going on here?* I pulled into the driveway on the side of the truck, and Simone pulled in behind me. Jumping out of the car, I approached a young man who was coming out of my home with the chair from Bryce's study. "Excuse me. Who are you, and what is going on here?" The young man held up his hands as if to ward me off.

"Look, ma'am, I don't want any trouble. My name is Billy. I'm from Gators Moving Company. I was called here today to pack up a couple of rooms. Anything else you need to know, you'll have to discuss that with Mr. Gordon." This wasn't this young man's fault. He was only doing his job.

"Thank you, Billy. I will discuss this with Mr. Gordon." Before going inside, I went to Simone's car.

She had already gotten out of the car and was standing against the door.

"Leah, what is going on here? Why is there a moving truck here?"

"I don't know. I'm going inside now to find out what this is all about. I need you to go on without me. And I don't know what's going to happen. I don't want the kids to see any of this. So if you don't hear from me before Bible study ends, just take the kids with you. I haven't said anything to my mother or Granny, and I don't want them asking me questions yet. Just make up something to tell them."

"Okay, but I really don't want to leave you."

"I will be just fine, Simone. Please do this. I don't want to have to worry about the kids too."

"I know, I know. I just want you to be okay."

"I will, and I'll call you if anything comes up, okay?"

"Okay, but seriously, you call me," Simone said, getting back into her car. I watched her pull off, and then I took a deep breath as I turned around and went inside the house.

"Bryce, where are you?" I called. There was no answer downstairs, so I climbed the stairs to our bedroom. And there he was sitting on the bed. When I walked in the room, he looked surprised to see me.

"Leah, what are you doing here? I thought you were going to church tonight."

"Oh, so while I'm supposed to be at church, you thought you would come and just pack up the house?" He stood up then and walked to the window.

"I'm not packing up the house, just *my* things."

"What? Are you moving out?"

"Yes, I am moving out. I was actually going to call you later and let you know." He'd been looking out the window as he talked. Now he turned and faced me. "I'm sorry, Leah, but I want out." As downhill as our marriage had gone, it was still extremely painful to hear him say these words to me. Some small part of me was still struggling to hold on.

"But you haven't even tried, Bryce. And now you say that you just want out? I don't understand this. I mean, it was just Sunday night that you were asking me for another chance. What's changed?"

"Leah, just drop it, okay."

"Just drop it? Ten years of marriage and just drop it? That's all you have to say to me?"

"Leah—"

"Just say it, Bryce, just say it."

"Okay, look, I probably won't file for a divorce right away, but I am leaving. I need to see what I want."

"That isn't what you started to say initially, so just say what you were going to say Bryce."

"I'm in love with her." All the energy drained out of me as he said those words. The last couple of days, I'd felt something wasn't right, and now he was telling me this. Feeling weak, I sat down on the bed.

"So you never really ended things with her at all?" I asked him quietly. He looked away from me then as his cell phone began to ring. He answered, and from the look on his face, I could tell it was her.

"I'm coming. No! Look, I'll be there in five minutes." He hung up with her, and still he refused to look at me.

"Leah, I've got to go. I'll call you sometime this week so we can figure out what we're going to tell the kids." Feeling angry again, I walked over to him, forcing him to look at me.

"So that's it, Bryce? She just calls and now you have to go? Is she your wife?" Grabbing me by the shoulders, Bryce pushed me away.

"I'm done discussing this with you. I want out, and that's it. I'm leaving," he said, and he walked out, leaving me in the room alone. Sinking to my knees, I began to cry out in pain.

"Lord, please, this is too much. Oh, Lord Jesus, please help me." For the second time within a week, I felt as if my heart was being ripped out. *Oh, God, how? How do I make it through this? Jesus, tell me what to do. Please, Lord. Please help.* Not knowing what to do with myself, I dragged myself to the bed. All I could do was lie there and cry. *Lord, please, I need you right now.*

Hours later I awoke, and the room was dark. Wondering what time it was, I looked over at the clock. I'd slept for two hours. How did I keep falling asleep during times like this? And then I remembered Pastor Richards's words. I sat up and reached for the phone. Simone picked up on the second ring. "Girl, I was just about to ride over there. Are you okay?"

"I'm not even going to lie to you. I am not okay, and I could really use someone to talk to." Before I knew it, I was crying again.

"Okay, that's it. I'm coming over there. Darren and Malaysia are asleep, but I'll just wake them up."

"No, don't wake them up. Let them sleep. I'll drive over there."

"Are you sure?"

"Yes, I'll come over there. I need something to do anyway."

"Okay, well bring the kids some clothes. Auntie Simone will keep them tonight, and I'll take them to school in the morning."

"Simone, what would I do without you?" She was so good to me.

"Fortunately for you, you'll never find out. Now hurry up and get over here."

Fifteen minutes later, I was sitting in Simone's condo. I'd checked on the children, and they were still sleeping. Now I was waiting on Simone, who was in the kitchen making us some hot tea. She returned from the kitchen with two steaming cups on a tray. She handed me a cup, took one for herself, and then sat down on the couch next to me. "So what happened?"

"He left me tonight. He says he wants out." I closed my eyes. I was so sick of crying. I couldn't believe how badly this hurt. "He said he's in love with her. I mean, I don't get it. Sunday night he was practically begging me for a second chance, and now he's gone to be with her. I can't pretend that we didn't have problems, but I thought we might at least try to work it out. I never imagined he'd fall in love with another woman. But then he said he wasn't filing for a divorce right away."

"So are you just supposed to wait while he decides which one of you he's going to choose?"

"I don't know, Simone. I just don't know." At a loss for words now, I drank some of my tea.

"So he never stopped seeing her at all. I don't know what to say. I'm just so sorry you're going through all of this." I looked at my friend, who looked so helpless.

"Thank you for just listening. I don't expect you to have the answers when I don't have the answers myself. I just need to clear my head, because I'm thinking of doing something major. I just need to make sure it's the right decision for me and for the children."

"What are you thinking of doing?"

"Well, I'm not going to sit around and wait while he's out doing whatever he wants with her. Honestly, our marriage has been going downhill for years, and I've been the only one trying. Despite all our other problems, this has really been the icing on the cake. So what I'm thinking is that I'm going to go ahead and file for divorce myself. Sunday I started a new beginning. Maybe this is all a part of that."

"Make sure that's what you really want to do."

"Oh, believe me, I will be praying about this situation heavily before I make a final decision. I just don't know what else to do if he says he wants out. And it hasn't been just a couple of weeks. I've been holding on much longer than that."

chapter 8

I sat back on the couch and got comfortable. "I really do appreciate you listening, but can we please talk about something else?"

"Are you sure?"

"Yes, I really need to focus on something else right now. So how was church?"

"I had a really good time. When I first got there, I was so worried about you that I could barely concentrate. But then the pastor actually started talking about worrying. That was the focus of Bible study. You know his daughter had been in that accident, but she is out of the coma, and the pastor says she is going to make a full recovery. You know we had to shout about that." I was glad to hear that Valerie was going to be okay. While the pastor and his wife were away, Granny and I had sent flowers and cards. And we'd prayed for Valerie's speedy recovery. "Anyway, he talked to us about when he and his wife arrived at the hospital to see their daughter. He said when they first saw her, Valerie had looked so small in that bed with all those tubes and machines. Pastor said when they saw that they both began to worry. But then he talked about how he just continued to pray, and then God gave Him peace.

"So he had us write everything that we were worried about on a piece of paper. There was this big basket, and once we wrote down the things that we were worried about, we had to put it in the basket. Then we prayed over it. And I knew that no matter what happened, you were going to be okay. We continued to pray, and I just let go and let God. By the end of the service, I decided it was time for me to stop hiding from God. I walked down that aisle. And, girl, you know Clara-Ann was shouting." I laughed when Simone said that because I could just see Granny now shouting all over the place. "So I joined the church, and now we're both members of Blessed Life Baptist Church. I really feel at home there." I was so happy for her.

"Simone, that is wonderful! I am so happy for you."

"I know. I'm happy about it too," she said, smiling.

"Okay, now let me totally flip the script. Leah, there was this tall, light-skinned, *fine* brother there at Bible study tonight. Lord, please forgive me, but I couldn't help but notice him."

"Let me ask you something. Does he have gray eyes?" Simone jumped up.

"Yes, who is he?" With a mind of its own, my heart skipped a beat.

"His name is Graye Barrington. He is actually Taylor's uncle."

"You mean *the* Graye Barrington? The one who owns Taylor Industries, the biggest conglomerate of construction companies on the east coast? That Graye Barrington? He's Taylor's uncle?"

"Yes."

"Well, girl he is—"

"I know, he's absolutely gorgeous," I said, cutting her off.

"Girl, are you okay? You look a little pale. Drink some more tea." To give myself something to do, I drank my tea. "So are you going to tell me what's up with this Graye Barrington or not?"

"There is really nothing to tell. Like you, the first time I saw him was at church. And then the other night, Taylor called with a family emergency. So I went over to her aunt's house, and he was there."

"So you've met him?"

"Yes, Simone, I met him." Simone plopped back down on the sofa.

"So what's he like? I mean, all the women in the church are talking about him and how he's the most eligible bachelor in Atlanta." I thought of the easy-going man I'd talked to a few days ago. I'd known he owned construction companies, but I hadn't known it was Taylor Industries. The company was widespread all over the country, and it employed thousands. Yes, Graye was rich, and yet, he seemed so down to earth, humble even. Great. Something else for me to like about him.

"Come on, Leah. Stop holding out on me. What is he like?" she asked, jumping up and down on the couch. I laughed at her. "You know, you're making me feel like I'm in high school again. Anyway, he seems like a genuinely nice person. You can tell he really loves Taylor."

"Mm-hmm."

I looked at her suspiciously. "Okay, now what is that supposed to mean?" She looked at me, her eyes sparkling, and I knew before she even spoke that she was up to no good.

"Don't you think that it's a strange coincidence that the new guy in town is Taylor's uncle, *your* Taylor? And he just so happens to be going to our church?"

"First of all, he's not new in Atlanta. He is from here. He moved away five years ago when his wife was killed in a car accident. And it *is* just a coincidence that he happens to be the uncle of my patient."

"Oh, so he's single?"

"I guess. I don't know. Why are you asking?" Simone held up her hands in mock defense.

"Hold on, girl. I don't want your man." Feeling embarrassed by the abruptness in my tone, I turned away. It wasn't my business who was interested in Graye. Once I was composed, I turned back to Simone. She was sitting there with her arms folded across her chest. And I could tell by the look on her face that I hadn't fooled her at all.

"He is not, nor will he ever be, my man. So let's get that straight right now. Have you forgotten the little fact that I'm a married woman? And have you also forgotten that his is the uncle of one of my patients? That in itself could mean a lot of trouble."

"No, I haven't forgotten any of those things. But I've known you for a long time, and I saw the look on your face when you said his name. And just to let you know, your voice also had this dreamy quality to it."

"It did not," I said, throwing a pillow at her.

"Yes, it did," she said, throwing the pillow right back. The next thing I knew we were into a full-fledged pillow fight. We were laughing and yelling as we whacked each other with pillows. I saw movement out of the corner of my eye and looked up and saw the kids standing in the hallway staring at us.

Simone and I stood there for a moment like school kids who had just gotten caught doing something wrong. Darren wiped his eyes as if to make sure he wasn't dreaming. Once he saw that he wasn't, he turned to Malaysia. "Come on, Laysia. Let's show them how a pillow fight is really done." They both ran and grabbed pillows. And then it was really on as the four of us laughed and attacked each other with pillows. There were pillow feathers all over the place.

Finally, breathless and tired, I yelled, "Stop." Simone, who was just as out of breath as I was, lay sprawled out on the floor.

"But, Ma, it was just getting good," Darren complained.

"That's as good as it's going to get. Now both of you go back bed while we clean this mess up."

Once the children were gone, Simone and I looked at each other and burst out laughing. "Can you believe that we were in here having a pillow fight?" I shook my head as I helped her up off the floor.

"Yes, I believe it. You know we all have that inner child inside of us somewhere. You have to admit it, though, you needed to laugh like that." I smiled at her as we cleaned up her living room.

"You're right. It was just what the doctor ordered. But seriously, Simone, don't you think I have enough drama going on without complicating things further?"

"Okay, I know you have a lot going on right now. I'm not trying to stress you out. I'm just pointing out the facts. You really did look excited when you talked about him."

"Did I?"

"Yes, you did."

"Okay, so I felt something when I met him. Big deal. I'm not going to act on it."

"What if he acts on it?"

"I'm pretty sure he knows I'm married. And I talked to him, Simone. He really does seem like he's a true man of God. So I don't think he would even approach me like that."

"Okay, so not now, but what if you do get divorced? Could you see anything happening then? I mean, men of God need love too."

"Oh, I am through with you. You are just too much. Listen, even though Bryce disrespected our marriage in the worst way, I'm not going to do the same thing."

"You don't have to convince me. I know you would never cheat on Bryce. But I just don't think that all this is a coincidence, and about three months from now, I'm going to remind you of this conversation," she said, shaking a finger at me.

"Fine."

"Fine."

Over the next three and a half weeks, I only saw Bryce once, when he came over to the house to tell the children that we were separating. It was one of the hardest things I'd ever had to do. Darren just sat there looking like he wanted to punch something or someone. Malaysia took it the hardest. She'd run from the room, crying. She didn't speak for the rest of the night.

Simone helped out a lot. She'd been over to the house almost every night. We did our best to take the kids' minds off everything, and for the most part, it seemed to work. Simone and I had also gotten involved in the church, and there were always things going on with the children and youth ministry. So that kept the children busy as well. School was going to end soon, and the church was preparing to conduct its very first summer camp. Everyone was excited about it. Simone and I had joined the youth ministry. The ministry had mostly everything set up for camp, but they'd been open to some new ideas that Simone and I had.

Being involved in the church wasn't just good for the children; it was the best thing for me as well. For one thing, it was strengthening my relationship with God. I'd never felt so close to Him. And it was in my brokenness that I truly saw how much I needed Him. Of course, being involved in the church meant that I had to see Graye all the time. He was part of the youth ministry as well. And of course, Simone continued to tease me about Graye. She said we stared at each other when we thought no one was looking. Every single woman in the church was trying to hook up with him, but he never seemed to be interested. Simone said it was because he was only interested in one woman, *me*. One Wednesday evening, after a church meeting, Graye approached me. "Leah, how are you doing?"

"I'm fine, Graye. How are you?"

"I'm good. I have a question for you?" My heart began to beat fast. As much as I didn't want to, I was going to have to let him down easy.

"Graye—"

"Leah, I want to know if I can pray for you."

"What?" I blinked, not sure I had heard him correctly.

"I'm asking you if I can pray for you."

"Well, yes, of course you can." I felt like a fool. I was glad he couldn't tell what I'd been thinking. He took my hand and began to pray.

"Lord, I come to You in prayer tonight, first of all just thanking You for being who You are. You are so worthy of all the praise. Lord, I'm praying for my friend Leah tonight. I pray that whatever she's going through, that you give her strength and peace, Father. Give her the comfort and the love that she needs. And, Jesus, let her know that as long as she has you, she is never alone. And lastly, Lord, guide her in the way that she should go, because with You as her guide, she will never be lost. Thank You, Lord. We praise your name, Jesus. These and many blessings, we ask in your name. Amen."

"Amen. Graye, thank you for that. I really needed that." I didn't know what else to say. Most days, I was holding up well. But today had just been one of those days. I kept having these flashes of sadness. But how had he known?

"There's no need to thank me, Leah. You have friends in Christ, and we are here for you. Always remember that. Have a good night, and I'll see you on Sunday."

"Good night, Graye."

I watched as he walked to his car. Simone walked up and stood beside me.

"Okay spill it, what was that all about? Did he ask you if he could take you to dinner?"

"No."

"Okay, well what's up?"

"He prayed for me." We both watched in silence as Graye left.

"That is deep, Leah."

"Yes, it was," I agreed. What he'd just done had truly touched me. No man besides a pastor had ever prayed for me. I would never forget this. And I didn't feel the sadness anymore. I felt the peace that Graye had prayed to God for. *Thank You, Lord.*

A few nights later, I was sitting in Granny's home. I called my mother and asked her to come as well. Once my mother got there, we all went into the kitchen to talk. Granny had taken it upon herself to cook a feast once she'd known we were all coming over. She had fried chicken, collard greens, macaroni and cheese, ham, dressing, sweet potato pie, her famous iced-tea, and my favorite, which I knew she'd made just for me, chocolate cake. She knew that I loved anything chocolate. I smiled as I sat down at the kitchen table. My grandmother had cooked like this all my life. Looking out the kitchen window, I could see that the kids were still running around in the yard playing. I cleared my throat and prepared myself. It was time to let them know what was going on. "Well, I just wanted to talk to the two of you and let you know what's going on." I watched as my mother and Granny exchanged a look. "Bryce and I are separated." And despite the many times I'd gone over this in my mind—what I was going to say and how I was going to say it, how I was going to be brave and not break down—I did exactly that. I broke down at the kitchen table. Granny walked over to me and put her arm around me.

"Let it out, child. Let it out." My mother reached for my hand across the table. Why had I been so afraid to tell my family? They loved me, and they would support me no matter what happened.

"Leah, we knew something was going on. We were just waiting for you to come to us. So do you want to tell us what happened?" my mother asked.

"He left me for another woman."

"I knew his eyes were shifty. My mama always said never trust a man with shifty eyes. That no good son of a gun."

"Calm down, Granny."

"Yeah, Mama, don't get your pressure up." Mama attempted to calm her down, even though I could tell by looking at her that she was upset herself. Granny went over to check on the food.

"I just always knew there was something about that man. Even when y'all moved into that big fancy house and had all that money, I still knew something wasn't right. That's why I wouldn't let him buy me *anything*." Granny slammed a spatula down on the counter.

"Granny!"

"I know, calm down, but I don't like my children being mistreated."

"I know, but I am going to be okay."

"So what are you going to do?" my mother asked.

"I don't know. I haven't even heard from him. He doesn't even call or come to see the kids. I'm thinking of filing for a divorce."

"Well, whatever you decide, we are here for you. Just make sure you pray about it."

"Oh, believe me, I have been."

"Okay, now let's get ready to eat. Get the children. My guests should be here any minute now."

"What guests, Granny?" I asked as I drank some tea.

"Oh, I invited the new deacon and his niece for dinner."

She hadn't. It just couldn't be. I felt a shiver go up my spine. "Um, what new deacon would that be?" I tried to hide the nervousness in my voice, but I was no match for my mother, who was looking at me as if she knew exactly what I was thinking. *Get it together, Leah. She can't possibly know what you're thinking or feeling right now.* "The name is Graye Barrington. Cynthia, have you seen him? He's a very nice-looking young man. And he has the nicest gray eyes."

He's coming here? No, it just can't be. Is it me or is it getting hot in here?

"No, Mama, I don't remember seeing him."

"He comes from a really good family. The Barringtons have always been good upstanding people. Graye used to be a member at the church years ago, but then his wife died and he moved away, poor thing. So I knew him from then. He was really involved in the church back then and always willing to lend a helping hand. Well, now he's moved back, and I told him that I was going to cook him a home-cooked meal. You know, it's just him and his niece now. Leah, what about you, have you met him yet?"

"Yes. Actually, his niece is one of my patients."

"Well, well, it sure is a small world," She said as she and my mother turned to look at me.

"Why are the two of you looking at me like that?"

"You tell us what's going on. All of a sudden you look like you're having a hot flash."

"Stop it, Mama. I do not." They continued to stare at me.

"Just how well do you know him, Leah?" my mother asked with an unreadable look on her face.

"Yeah, what's up with that?"

Simone was bad enough. Now I was going to have to hear it from these two. And they were ganging up on me.

We all looked outside as Graye pulled up in a Chrysler 300. *Just how many cars does he have?* Standing up, I made up a flimsy excuse. "I have to go to the bathroom," I said as I left the kitchen. I could still hear them talking about me.

"What is wrong with that girl, Cynthia? And why is she making a general announcement about going to the bathroom? I tell you, young folks these days. I just don't know about them sometimes."

"I don't know either, Mama, but let's go and greet our guests."

While they went off to greet Graye and Taylor, I went to the bathroom to get myself together. Once inside the bathroom, I closed and locked the door. I breathed a sigh of relief, until I saw my appearance in the mirror. I looked flushed, as if I'd just finished running. And this happened every time Graye's name was mentioned. And if he was around, you could just hang it up, because I was a nervous wreck. All my life I'd been confident, assertive; this was something I just wasn't used to. I just didn't understand this at all. If it was just a physical attraction, I'd be able to deal with it better. But whenever I was around him, it always felt like there was something deeper going on, which was crazy because we hardly knew each other. But when he looked at me and I looked at him, there was this connection that just seemed so real. It was as though we were talking without actually saying words. We never spoke of it; it just hung in the air every time we were around each other. And I just knew that Granny and my mother would be able to see it. And why not? I hadn't fooled Simone at all. Deep in thought, it took a moment for it to register in my mind that someone was knocking on the door.

"Ma, we're all ready to eat. We're just waiting on you. Are you okay in there?" It was Darren. Finally admitting to myself that I could not hide in the bathroom all night, I opened up the door.

"I'm fine, Darren. Let's go eat." I was just going to have to put on a good show. *I can do this. I will do this,* I told myself.

"Hello, everyone," I said, greeting them as cheerfully as I could. I was going to make the best of this situation and not embarrass myself. Taylor jumped up, hugging me around the waist.

"Hey, Dr. Leah."

"How are you, Taylor?" I asked as I returned the hug.

"I'm great. Uncle Graye's here, you're here." I watched Taylor as she went back to her seat. I could see that Graye's presence in her life was really making a positive difference. She was communicating, smiling, and not afraid anymore to be around people.

"Hello, Leah." I knew the voice without even having to look.

"Hello, Graye. How are you?"

"I'm good, and yourself?"

"Hungry," I said, sitting down next to Malaysia. My gaze swept across the table at all the food. Granny had really thrown down today. Everyone was talking and laughing as we all waited to get started. Granny cleared her throat to get our attention.

"Graye, would you please lead us into a word of prayer?" Bowing my head as Graye blessed the food, I was reminded of when he'd prayed for me. I felt comforted every time I thought of that evening and what he'd said after.

"Amen," he concluded.

"Amen," we all responded, and then we began our feast.

For the next hour, we ate, talked, and laughed. This was exactly what I had needed, to be with family. And I was doing so well. Whenever Graye asked me a question, I didn't look at him directly. I refused to be hypnotized by his eyes today. But I had to admit, even though I wasn't looking him in the eyes, his voice had an effect on me as well. But I remained calm. I was determined not to embarrass myself. I smiled and continued to relax. I was pulling this off, and most importantly, Granny and my mother didn't suspect a thing. "Okay, everyone, now it's time for dessert." Granny brought out sweet potato pie and chocolate cake. "Now, everyone is welcome to some sweet potato pie, but you'll have to ask Leah about the chocolate cake, because I made it especially for her," Granny said, giving me a wink.

Chocolate, I dramatically reached for my cake as if it were a long-lost friend, and everyone laughed at my antics.

After dessert, the kids went back outside to play, while all the adults stayed inside for kitchen duty. It wasn't a full minute before Darren was running back inside. "Hey, Graye, we've got some friends from the neighborhood who want to play some football. Do you want to play?" Graye turned to the rest of us, his gray eyes pleading. It was absolutely ridiculous for a man to be this fine. Granny playfully swatted at Graye.

"Oh, who's going to say no to you with those eyes? Get out of here. But next time, you will have kitchen duty, young man," she said, shaking her finger at him. In a flash, he was out the door with Darren. No one spoke for a moment.

"Well, Darren seems to be on a first-name basis with Mr. Barrington," my mother observed. I had noticed that as well, and I had to admit that even though I wasn't seriously concerned, it did worry me a little. These days Bryce wasn't around, and as angry as Darren was right now, Bryce was the only father figure Darren had ever known. I didn't want him getting hurt by getting too attached to another man we hardly knew.

"And I've seen Darren following him around church," I heard my mother say.

"Oh, leave them alone. That boy needs a positive male in his life. I've known Graye for years, and he is a good man. And you know what makes him even better?" Granny asked. "He's a true man of God. Did y'all know that last week he took a few of the church members and flew to Virginia to check on the pastor and his family? He paid for their flights and hotel accommodations and everything. Pastor Richards hadn't even asked him to come, but he wanted the pastor and his family to feel the love and support of the church. And he is getting ready to do some major expansions on the church. It will include expanding the church itself and a youth center, school, gym, and other things we've always wanted for our children. So y'all leave my friend alone now."

My mother held up her hands in mock surrender. "Okay, Mama, I'm backing up off your friend," she said, laughing.

"That's right, back up off him now." Granny was laughing as well. I smiled, shaking my head at them. Loading the last dish in the dishwasher, I decided to take a break.

"I'll be back. I'm going to check on the kids," I told them.

"Mama, you know who she's really checking on," my mom said, and they both burst out laughing as I left the kitchen.

Sitting down on the porch swing, I watched the kids. Malaysia and Taylor were in the next-door neighbors' yard, talking and laughing with the neighbor's daughter. For a moment, Malaysia looked older than her nine years. These children were growing up too fast. I looked over at Darren and Graye, who were playing football with some teenagers from the neighborhood. My son was taller than me now, and he was only thirteen. I watched as Darren laughed at something Graye said. My son's biological father had been absent most of Darren's life. Every now and then, he came around and tried to play Daddy, but it was never long before he'd start making empty promises to my son. Bryce was the only father Darren had ever really known. And now he wasn't showing my son any love. Darren seemed okay, but I knew he missed Bryce, and that was a void I was still trying to figure out how to fill. I had tried to call Bryce. I left him messages, asking him to call or come see the children. Most of the time he never answered. Whenever he did decide to return my message and call back, he was always too busy to see them. I just didn't know what to do anymore.

I watched as Graye threw the football to Darren and my baby scored a touchdown. I almost stood up and clapped, but I knew Darren wouldn't want his mother to do that in front of his boys. On one hand, Darren talking to Graye could be a good thing. I'd seen Graye talk to the youth in our church before. They really liked him because he kept it real, and at the same time he found a way to incorporate the spiritual aspect of the situation, whatever the situation was. And Darren really could use a positive male role model right about now. I just didn't want Darren to get overly attached. I didn't want my son's feelings to be hurt if one day Graye couldn't be there for him.

Now they were both waving at me. I waved back. I closed my eyes and sat back in the swing and rocked back and forth.

chapter 9

Today had really been a good day, and I'd learned something as well. I'd learned two things actually. Being a psychologist, I'd helped so many patients face the truth and deal with how they really felt, but I hadn't taken my own advice. It had been there all the time, but to admit it meant I had to deal with it. Looking back now, I could see how I'd been in denial about my marriage. Over the years, our problems had continued to grow and grow. I had tried to deal with them, but when Bryce refused to try at all, I simply helped him sweep them under the rug. The downfall of our marriage was both of our faults. But now he'd committed the ultimate betrayal. I was done waiting and sick of trying all by myself. I had to face it once and for all; we were over.

When I'd seen Graye for the first time, I'd instantly felt a connection. But I'd basically chalked it up to the fact that I was going through hell in my marriage. Yes, at first, I thought this had to be some kind of a rebound. But now I realized what it was that made me so nervous when I was around him. The way I felt when I was around him, the connection every time we looked at each other, I'd never felt like this before. Not even with Bryce, the man I'd given eleven years of my life to. No man had ever stirred these kinds of feelings inside of me. And now that I had admitted this to myself, I could deal with this. And I would deal with it by not doing anything at all. I knew now that my marriage was over and I was going to file for a divorce, but that didn't mean that I was ready for a relationship. If and when I did get involved with another man, it would be a long time from now. In time, these feelings that I was having for Graye would fade, I was sure.

"You're just not going to make this easy for me, are you?" Startled by the sound of Graye's voice, I jumped up from the swing.

"What? How long have you been standing there?"

"I'm sorry. I came over here to talk to you, but you were just looking so incredibly beautiful that I just watched you for a moment. Okay, maybe that sounds corny, but it's the truth."

He just called me beautiful. He was standing there, looking like an absolute dream. And though he'd been playing football, he looked as if he'd hardly broken a sweat. *Oh, why does he have to be so gorgeous? And what did he mean by that first comment? Keep it together, girl.* "Thank you for the compliment, Graye. What's up?"

Graye sat down on the porch steps. "I'm not sure if Taylor told you or not, but five years ago, I lost my wife. In my grief, I closed myself off from everything and everyone, and I ran. I ran away from Atlanta, but most importantly, I ran away from God. I spent days, weeks, months, years in denial about how much I was hurting. And I think a part of me even blamed God. I hid in my work, my companies. I made all the money in the world and then some. All the while, deep inside, I was empty and hurting. And then a year ago I lost my sister, and I thought I would die. It was like losing a part of myself. I finally broke. And in my complete brokenness, I called His name. And He came and He saved me. This past year, God has given me peace about so many things. And one thing I learned is how to be honest with myself and what I was feeling. I'm done with denial. That being said, I have to admit that I'm starting to have feelings for you." I felt an excited shiver go up my spine at his words.

"I felt something so powerful the very first time I saw you. It rocked me because, one, it wasn't sexual. Yes, you're a beautiful woman." He looked away for a moment, and when he turned back, the look in his eyes was so intense I forgot everything around us. "But, Leah, it was more than that, more than an attraction. It was unlike anything I've ever felt. I mean, I truly loved Carrie. She was my high-school sweetheart. But even with her, I'd never felt this. Do you know what it felt like?" If it was at all possible, his eyes became even more intense. I was hypnotized and utterly powerless against the emotions raging inside me.

"It felt like coming home. After a long journey of hurt and pain, I looked at you and the sun shined again, and all I could think was *home*." He became silent then. My heartbeat quickened as our eyes locked. I was dreaming. This beautiful man was saying exactly what I'd been feeling. Looking away, I fought with emotions I wasn't ready to deal with yet. No man had ever said anything so deep, so profound to me before. "Tell me, Leah, did you feel that too?" I looked at this man who was unlike any man I'd ever met before in my life. There was no point in me lying to him after he'd been so completely honest with me.

"Yes, Graye, I feel it too." He smiled then, but I could still see some emotion in his eyes.

"Thank you for that. It felt so strong that at times I wondered if I really was losing my mind." I laughed when he said that.

"That's the same thing I thought about myself."

"Well, at least now I know it's not all in my mind," he said, laughing with me. Then he grew serious once again.

"Then I found out you were married, and I admit, I was really disappointed. I mean, Taylor had only mentioned you. Anyway, I don't want us tiptoeing around each other. Yes, I feel this way about you, but I also respect you, Leah. And I will never disrespect your marriage by trying to take things any further. I promise you that. I just don't want to avoid you, and I don't want you to feel that you have to avoid me. I can accept the fact that you're married and I can't have you, but please don't make me accept the fact that we can't at least be friends."

"Do you really think that we can be friends with these feelings that we have for each other?"

"Well, I'd like to at least try. If we try and it doesn't work, I'll accept that. But can we try?" He gave me his best puppy dog look. I had no choice but to laugh he looked so pitiful. He was always doing that, making me laugh. There it was, one more thing for me to like about him.

I could tell him right now that I had decided to end my marriage, but where would that leave us? I still wasn't ready for a relationship. Who knew if I ever would be? There was no point in giving him any false hope. I stared at him for a moment. This beautiful man could have any woman he wanted, and he wanted me. I had to admit it, I was flattered. Still, it was best if I didn't tell him about my plans for a divorce. Maybe we really could be friends. "Okay, Graye, we'll give it a try." The smile on his face made me want to jump off the swing and into his arms. But I guess that wouldn't be a good start for our friendship. *Lord, give me strength. Please.*

We both turned to look as we heard the kids. It was Malaysia and Taylor. Darren was still playing football. The two girls walked toward us, and the looks on their faces told me all I needed to know. They were up to something. Graye looked at me. He knew they were up to something too. Once they stood in front of us, Taylor pushed Malaysia in front of her. So my child was going to be the spokesperson of the group. "Mom, we were wondering if we could spend the night here with Grandma."

"If it's okay with Grandma, I don't mind. You'll just have to ask her." Taylor turned to Graye then.

"Uncle Graye, can I stay?" Graye, suddenly looking a little nervous, looked at me for help.

"Hey, why don't you all go inside and ask Granny. Taylor, let me talk to your uncle for a minute. Okay?"

"Okay," she said reluctantly as she followed the other two inside. Once they were gone, I turned my attention to Graye.

"Okay, what's wrong?"

"Well, you know Taylor just moved in with me, and she hasn't spent the night out yet. It makes me nervous, I mean what if she gets scared in the middle of the night and wants to come home?" I'd never seen any man look so gorgeous and worried at the same time, but here he was doing it.

Focus, stay focused. "Okay, Graye, I know you're new to the whole parenting thing, so let me clue you in on a few things. The first thing is that Taylor is thirteen, not four or five. If, for some reason, she decides she wants to go home, she knows exactly how to contact you. But judging from the way she's hit it off with my children, especially Malaysia, I don't think she'll be calling you. And let me say this, Granny is not one of those people who lets children run wild and crazy when they stay over. Oh, they'll have food and plenty of fun, but my kids will tell you, Granny doesn't play, and she checks on the kids and her house several times a night. So stop worrying. And this is good for Taylor. I mean, there's a few years in age difference, but have you seen the way Taylor and Malaysia have already bonded? Taylor hasn't interacted with people outside her immediate circle in a long time; she's really coming around." He looked less nervous now.

"You're right. She is slowly but surely coming out of that shell. In fact, everything you're saying is true. I guess I get nervous sometimes. This is still new to me, and I really just want to be a good parent."

"You are going to be a wonderful parent. If you ever have any questions, you know I'll be here. I love that little girl too."

"I know, and I am very grateful for that." Just then, Malaysia and Taylor came running outside.

"She said yes," they both said at the same time.

"Uncle Graye?" Taylor questioned.

"Okay, yes, that's fine, Taylor. Go tell Clara-Ann that I'm taking you to get some clothes." The girls, excited about being able to stay together tonight, ran back inside the house to relay the message. Graye stood up and brushed off his pants.

"Well, Darren and I probably won't be here when you get back, so I'll see you tomorrow. Granny keeps clothes here for Malaysia, so she's all set." The girls came back outside, and I could tell by looking at Taylor's face that she was ready to go get those clothes and get back here as soon as possible. "You girls be good," I said, hugging them both. After hugging me, Taylor grabbed her uncle's arm and began pulling him toward the car.

"Have a good night, Leah."

"Good night, Graye." I peeked my head inside the front door. "Granny, Mama, I'm getting ready to leave." They both came outside to say good-bye.

"Malaysia, why don't you go make sure the guest-room is all set up for you and Taylor."

"Okay, Grandma." I knew that room was just fine. I shook my head. They were up to something.

"So, Leah, I noticed you talking to Graye." My mother was determined to find out what the deal was between us.

"Yes, we had a nice conversation, nothing major." My mother looked at Granny and rolled her eyes. The fact that Graye and I had admitted to having feelings for each other was definitely major, but I wasn't going to share that with these two. I didn't care how many times my mother rolled her eyes. Besides, we were keeping things on a friendship level, so no one needed to know anything. *We can handle this. I hope.* "Darren, wrap it up, it's time to go," I said, yelling so he could hear me. Darren, who had been talking to some friends, came running over to us. Good, I was saved by the bell.

"We're leaving?"

"Yes, Malaysia and Taylor are staying here with Granny.

"Aw man."

"Don't 'aw man' me. You know you're not staying the night out anywhere this weekend. You've got to finish your science project. This is it. School will be over in another week."

"I've been meaning to talk to you about that, Leah." Granny stopped for a moment. "Darren, go inside with your sister, please. I need to talk to your mother."

She continued once he was gone. "When school ends next week, I know the kids are going to start at the church camp. But I wanted you to let them stay over here with me this summer. They'll still go to camp, and over here, you know they have friends to keep them busy. But the main reason is you. I know for our sake you were really trying to hold yourself together when you told us what was going on with Bryce. But I can see that this thing has torn you up inside. You can take this time and decide what you really want to do. All I'm trying to say is that you need some you time. So what do you say?" They had stayed the summer before, and I knew that they'd had a good time. I'd still seen them all the time because I'd been over here a lot myself. What she was saying made perfectly good sense. It was just that Bryce had left me, and now it felt like my children were leaving me too. I was overdramatizing and I knew it, but I couldn't help it.

"I don't know, Granny. Let me think about it. I'll let you know by next week."

"Okay, fair enough."

On the way home, I listened as Darren told me play-by-play how his team had won the football game. I thought this might be the perfect opportunity to really talk to him. After he was done talking about the game, I turned the volume down on the music. "So, Darren, how are *you* doing?" Darren gave me a weird look, like I knew he would. Sometimes talking to my own teenage son was harder than talking to a patient for the first time.

"I'm fine, Ma."

"Darren, I know there have been a lot of changes lately. I just want you to know that if you have any questions or if you need to talk, I am here to listen."

"Ma, stop worrying. I'm straight. Sometimes I talk to Deacon Graye."

"Darren, what did you tell him?" I asked, panicking.

"Oh, not about that. We just talk about guy stuff." I breathed a sigh of relief when I realized he hadn't told Graye about what was going on between Bryce and me.

I was actually glad that Darren was talking to some-one, even if it was "just guy stuff." Bryce didn't call or come around to see the kids at all, so it was easy to see Darren talking to Graye. But all the kids seemed to gravitate toward Graye. He really had a gift with the youth. "That's cool that you have someone to talk to, Darren. Just know that you have your mom too."

"Okay. Ma?" This was it, one of those shining moments in a parent's life. My son was going to confide in his mother.

"Yes, Darren?"

"Can you please turn the music back up?"

When we got home, I sat down to relax once the kids were settled. I didn't have to worry about dinner, because Granny had taken care of that today. I decided to call Simone to see what she was up to. She answered on the third ring, sounding out of breath. "Hey, what's up? How was your day today?" I thought of my decision about Bryce and the talk with Graye. It had truly been a day of revelation.

"I had a good day. We all went to Granny's for dinner. But what I want to know is why you're so out of breath."

"I was workin' it out, girl. Workin' it out."

"Oh, do you want me to call you back?"

"Oh no, you don't get off that easy. I was told that a certain fine, light-skinned brother was seen in Clara-Ann's yard today." I couldn't believe it. As big as Atlanta was, Simone still found out *everything*. Well, there was no sense in denying it.

"Yes, Simone. I didn't even know she had invited them until I saw them pull up in the yard."

"You said 'them.' Who else was there?"

"Taylor came with Graye."

"Mm-hmm. So it was like one big happy family? I can't believe this, I mean what are the odds? There's no way that you can tell me now that it's just a coincidence the two of you just keep bumping into each other."

"Well, what I will say is that we talked today, I mean really talked." I could hear the excitement in my voice, but I couldn't even stop myself. "Simone, he even admitted that he is starting to have feelings for me."

"I knew it! knew there was something between you two. So what's up? What are you going to do?"

"Nothing. He was so sweet about the whole thing. And I have to admit I do feel something. But I'm not ready for anything, and I don't know if I ever will be. We just agreed to be friends."

"Leah?"

"What?" I could hear the smirk in her voice.

"Leah?"

"*What!*"

"Do you really think with the chemistry the two of you have that you're going to be able to be just friends?"

"We're going to at least try. Anyway, there is something else that I have to tell you. I've decided to go ahead with the divorce. And before you ask, it has nothing to do with Graye. Yes, I am attracted to him, and yes, it feels like it could even be something deeper, but my decision has nothing to do with him."

"Well, I know it couldn't have been an easy decision to make. What was the deciding factor?"

"No, it wasn't an easy decision to make, and I didn't rush it. I have been praying about it and just waiting for an answer. Today, it became so clear to me as I was sitting there with my family. We were just eating and having a good time. We talked and laughed. It just felt like family. And I realized that at home it hasn't been like that with Bryce, not for a long time. Even the kids are used to him being gone. Initially, they were upset when he left, but they've adjusted so well. And you know why? It's because he disappeared years ago. Mentally, he just dropped out of our lives. And I can't make him be here if he wants to go. I have my children, you, Granny, Mama, and the rest of my family. I'll make it through this, and I'll be just fine. We all will."

"And don't forget you've got Jesus too."

"Oh no, I can't forget that. See, I had to come back to Him first. And when I did, that's when I began to feel peace. Before I even made up my mind on what I was going to do, I felt peace. And in this situation, with all this drama, it can't be nobody but Jesus that's keeping me together."

"Amen to that, sista!"

"So do you know anyone?"

"Anyone like who?"

"A good divorce lawyer?"

Monday morning, I pulled into the Southpoint Business Park. My appointment was at 9:00 a.m., and it was just 8:45. I got out of the car and stood looking toward my destination. The sign on the building read, "Veronica Sanchez, Attorney at Law." Simone said she was one of the best divorce lawyers in Atlanta, an absolute genius in the courtroom. She was a fighter who kept the opposition on its toes. And with her honesty and fairness, she'd earned the respect of many of her peers. So here I was. Strangely enough, I wasn't nervous at all. Once I'd made the appointment, I wasn't sure how I would actually react once I got here. But to my surprise, I was fine; I was at peace. Grabbing my purse and locking up the car, I headed toward the building. Once inside, I walked to the front desk. The receptionist smiled at me.

"Good morning. How may I help you?"

"Yes, good morning. I have a nine o'clock appointment with Veronica Sanchez."

The receptionist typed away at her computer. "Mrs. Gordon?"

"Yes."

"Thank you. Mrs. Sanchez will be with you in just a moment. If you will, please make yourself comfortable." She gestured toward the comfortable-looking chairs.

"Thank you," I said as I walked to the nearest chair. I sat down and surveyed my surroundings. The neutral browns and earth tones gave the room a calming feel.

And despite the nature of this business, the office provided a friendly atmosphere for the potential client.

"Mrs. Gordon?"

"Yes," I answered, standing.

"Mrs. Sanchez will see you now. It's the first room on the left, number eight oh eight."

"Thank you." I walked down the hall to the room. Knocking softly, I waited until I heard a voice on the other end.

"Please, come in." I walked in and was greeted by a petite, pretty, middle-aged woman. She stood up as I walked in and held out her hand. As we shook hands, she flashed me with what I would soon come to know as her winning smile. "Please take a seat, Mrs. Gordon. Make yourself comfortable," she offered. I sat down, and for the first time, I felt like the patient. "So, how can I help you today?" She was straightforward, and I appreciated that.

"Mrs. Sanchez, I am here to file for a divorce."

Hours later, I was sitting in my own office. I had just finished with a new patient. Brooke buzzed me. "Dr. Gordon?"

"Yes? What's up, Brooke?"

"Um, I noticed that you have some time. I was wondering if I could talk to you for a moment."

"Sure, what can I help you with?"

"Well, I was going to come to your office." I realized she wanted to *really* talk to me.

"That's no problem Brooke, come on in."

"Okay, I'll be there in a minute." I wondered what was bothering her. But I'd find out in just a minute. While waiting, my mind drifted back to my previous conversation with Veronica Sanchez. We'd hit it off immediately. I already liked her and had decided to hire her. During this initial consultation, we'd talked a lot about my marriage and why I wanted the divorce. And she'd wanted to know how I wanted to proceed as far as our assets and custody. One of the first steps would be for Bryce to get served divorce papers. That was the only thing that worried me. I had no idea how he was going to react. I thought back to the night we'd fought. I didn't want to go through anything like that ever again. I'd been so out of control, and so had he. I wanted things to end nicely and neatly, but something told me that he wasn't going to make this easy.

It was hard to believe that it had all come to this. Bowing my head, I said a short prayer for Bryce and myself. *Lord, please forgive me for ending my marriage, and please give us the strength to get through this. Lord, help me to forgive Bryce and keep me from being bitter. And thank You, Father. Thank You for this peace You have given me. Amen.* I heard a soft knock on the door. "Come in, Brooke." Brooke walked in and sat down on the couch.

"I guess I'm the patient today."

"Brooke, you know you can talk to me anytime, so what's up?"

"I don't even know where to start, Dr. Gordon. My life is a mess. Okay, you know I've been with Justin for a year now. Everything was great, and last year when I came into some money, I let him talk me into buying a house. We've made plans—you know, marriage, kids, the whole nine. Well, about a week and a half ago, I went to the doctor and I found out that I am pregnant. And basically, overnight, Justin changed."

Brooke stood up then and began to pace. She reminded me of myself as she walked around my office trying to make sense out of something that just didn't make sense. "I mean it's as if he's this completely different person. He won't talk to me, and all of a sudden he comes home late. And this morning when I got up for work, I found this." Her voice shook as she took out what looked to be a note. She began to read it to me.

"Dear Brooke, I love you, and everything was fine until you went and got pregnant. I am not ready to be a father. I can't handle this, so I've decided that I'm leaving. There is some money on the counter for bills for the next month. After that, you're on your own. I'm sorry it had to go down like this, but I refuse to be trapped into something that I don't want. Besides, how do I even know that the baby is mine? I've moved all my things from the house, and please don't try to find me. It's over. Justin." This felt like déjà vu. I walked around from my desk and sat down on the couch across from Brooke.

For a moment, we both sat there in silence. I shook my head in disbelief at Justin's hurtful words in the letter. "I am so sorry that this has happened to you. I want you to know from the beginning, no matter what Justin does or doesn't do, I am going to be here for you." Seeing the pain and shock in her face and once again, I had the feeling of déjà vu. "I know you love him, and that's the part that hurts so much. Because when you're in love with a man, even when that man hurts you, the love doesn't just go away. As much as we hurt and wish we didn't care or love them anymore, it just doesn't work that way." Pastor Richards's words flashed in my mind: "*Share what you're going through. Be real and reach out to each other in love.*"

I settled back into the couch to get comfortable. "Brooke, I'm going to share some things with you because I want you to know that you're not out there by yourself. I met my first love, Derrick, in the ninth grade. We were both so young. I got pregnant with Darren in my junior year, and it was hard. I was still living at home with my mother, but most of the responsibility was on me. I was basically a child with a child. Derrick and I tried to stay together, and we made plans to be a family, and for a while I really believed it was going to happen. But it wasn't long before Derrick was tired of being Daddy. We started fighting all the time, and it wasn't long before he just completely left. I was left to struggle with Darren on my own. By the grace of God, I made it to college. And, girl, I am telling you, having a son and trying to go to school was the biggest challenge I'd ever faced. But I will tell you one thing: it made me strong. So that was my past, now let me fast forward to the present. Can you guess where I was this morning?"

"No, where were you?"

"I went to see a divorce lawyer." I watched Brooke look at me first in surprise, and then concern registered on her face. "I am okay, and I am at peace," I said, giving her hand a reassuring pat. "But that didn't happen overnight. It takes time to get to that point. I just want you to know that while you're getting to that point, Simone and I will be here to help you along the way."

"Thank you, Dr. Gordon. It really does help to know that I am not the only one going through this. But are you sure you're going to be okay?"

"I'm going to be just fine. But I didn't think so at first. See, I truly loved my husband. I still do in some ways. I loved that man so much that for years I fought all by myself, trying to save my marriage. But the truth of it is, you can't fight all by yourself, and my marriage has been on a downward spiral for years now. Recently, I found out that Bryce has been having an affair, and I was forced to confront the truth that I'd been so desperately trying to hide from. For weeks I cried, asking myself why this was happening to me. I still don't know why yet, but I have come to the realization that it is truly over between Bryce and me. And now I feel peace with the decision that I've made.

"Now, our situations may not be the same. But the hurt and the pain of the situation are similar. And I know you feel a sense of betrayal the same way I do. You've loved Justin and made plans with him. And now that there is going to be a baby, he has totally flipped the script on you. And now you're left wondering what you're going to do. And I've realized some things these last couple of months. As women, we love with everything in us." Sighing, I thought of all the love I'd put into my marriage. "Maybe that's the mistake right there. If we're loving them with everything we have in us, then what do we have left for ourselves? What can we give God? Once that man is in our heart, we give all we can to that man and that relationship. And when they break our heart, we fall so hard. The pain of it becomes almost unbearable." Brooke nodded her head in agreement. She was trying so hard to keep it together. She was young, but she was strong.

"I feel your pain, but we are going to get through this. And hey, we're going to have a little baby around the office." We both laughed then, and Brooke placed her hand on her stomach. "This baby is a gift from God, Brooke, and it's going to receive so much love from all of us. Justin may have walked away, but you're not alone. You have love and support from me and from Simone," I told her as I gave her a hug. "Okay?"

"Thank you, Dr. Gordon. I really needed to hear this." A single tear escaped from her eyes.

"Whenever you need to talk, I am here. Now if you need a babysitter, call Simone," I said, laughing.

"Hey, what's so funny in here?" Simone poked her head inside my office door. As she stepped into the office, Brooke and I looked at each other and laughed again as we tried to imagine Simone with baby bottles and diapers.

"Are you okay now?" I asked Brooke as she stood up.

"Yes, I am good. I really needed this. Thank you. I really feel as if a weight has been lifted. I am lucky to have you and Dr. Lloyd."

"We are lucky to have you. You know you keep this place going."

"Amen on that," Simone agreed. "Now, can the two of you fill me in on what you were laughing at?" I should've known my friend wasn't going to let that one slide. I looked at Brooke. This was her story, and I wasn't going to betray her trust.

"It's okay. I trust you both. I've got to get back up front, so I will leave you to explain the details to Simone." She closed the door softly as she left. Once she was gone, Simone plopped down on my sofa.

"Is she okay? What's going on?"

chapter 10

For the next few minutes, I filled Simone in on the details. Once I'd told her everything, she sat there in silence for a moment, just shaking her head. "That's what makes me mad about men. One minute they're telling you how much they love you and how they'll always be there for you, and then when that's put to the test, they shut down and bail out. The woman is just left alone to pick up the pieces. We're going to have to be there for her and that baby. And what about her family?"

"I think her mother is still alive, but other than that, she doesn't have a lot of family." Simone stood up and walked around the office. Between the three of us, we were wearing some floors out.

"I just can't stand selfish men who refuse to take care of their responsibilities."

"Well, I already told her that we'll be there for her. You're right about one thing: there are some selfish men out there. But you know what, Simone? As much as I'm going through in my own situation, I would still like to believe that there are some good ones out there—men of honor who stand by their word and mean exactly what they say."

Simone, who had been lounging on the couch, sat up straight then and looked at me. "I can't believe it. After everything you've been through these last few months, you're still a hopeless romantic."

"Yes, I admit it, I still believe in love. Maybe one day I—"

"Maybe one day you and Graye will be together."

"That's not what I was going to say."

"But you've thought about it, admit it."

"Okay, so maybe I've entertained the idea once or twice. But like I told you before, I'm not ready for anything like that yet."

"Yeah, we'll see. You can't fool me. I've seen you the way the two of you look at each other. And there's something else. When you're both in the same room, there is just this energy. And I know that you're attracted to each other, but it just seems like it's even more than that." My heart skipped a beat as I thought of Graye and the connection I felt with him.

Friends, remember that, Leah. Just friends, I told myself. Now if I could just believe that.

"Well, you know I don't usually let you off the hook this easily, but I have to change the subject. What happened when you went to see Veronica Sanchez?"

"Well, first let me say thank you for recommending her. We hit it off right away. We talked about filing for a divorce and basically everything that goes along with it. She says divorces like ours can sometimes get a little complicated because of all the assets."

"By complicated, you mean who's going to get this and who's going to get that?"

"Exactly. She said some people are so consumed with anger and regret that they'll fight over anything. She said she's seen people battle it out over a pillow."

"A pillow?"

"A pillow. I stressed to her how much I do not want this divorce to be like that. I told her the truth, though. Bryce can be very vindictive when he wants to be. All I want is my car and the house in West Palm Beach. Our children have always loved that place. We can sell the main house, and everything else, he can have it. Simone, I prayed about it, and I asked God to forgive me for getting a divorce, and He has. When I stepped into Veronica Sanchez's office, I felt total peace. I truly feel that I'm doing what's best for myself and for my children."

"I can tell. I don't hear any hesitation in your voice, and I don't see any regret when I look at you. And I can just feel the peace. So what happens now?"

"Veronica says the next step is Bryce getting served. It's the only thing I'm worried about. I have no idea how he's going to take this. I know he doesn't want me, but he likes to be the one in control. I told you what he said. Even while he was telling me he was leaving me, he was still saying he wasn't going to file for a divorce right now, as if he was the only who had a choice. I just know he's not going to like that fact that I've taken matters into my own hands."

"You don't think that fool will try anything, do you?"

"I don't know. I would like to think he wouldn't, but things have been so out of control. This entire situation has brought out parts of us that I'm sure neither one of us has ever seen before."

"Well, if you need me to come over, I will. Or if you want to come with the kids, you know you're more than welcome."

"I know, thank you. I might just have to take you up on that."

Two days later, I walked into the office to see a smiling Brooke. "Well, good morning, Brooke. I am loving that smile on your face."

"And I am happy to be smiling. I had my first prenatal visit this morning. You know, ever since I told Justin about the baby, it's been rough. I was caught off guard with his response. But today, when I heard my baby's heartbeat for the first time, I just knew that everything was going to be okay. I have to admit that despite Justin's letter, I did try to reach him. He changed his number. I called his mother's house to see if he was there. He had already told her the situation. And you know what, she told him that if he couldn't take responsibility for this baby, than he couldn't stay at her house. She told me from the moment she met me she liked me. She says she can tell right away what a person is all about."

"She sounds like my grandmother Clara-Ann." Looking at Brooke, I could see there was still some sadness, but I also saw hope.

"She says she's going to be here for me and her first grandchild. I am still hurt, and I still love Justin. But I am glad that I saw the real Justin. I mean, I was with him for almost two years, and I really thought I knew him, but obviously I didn't really know him at all.

"Anyway, his mother is being really supportive, and I appreciate that. When I called my mother, she immediately wanted me to move back home. And that is an option that I have, but I love Atlanta, I love my job, and I just refuse to let Justin run me out of town. His mother says after she told him about taking responsibility, they got into it really bad and he left. She says she hasn't heard from him in days. And I've decided I am not going to chase him around trying to make him do the right thing. I just hope he eventually comes around for our child. It's too late for the two of us, but I really want him to have a relationship with his child."

"Brooke, I hope he comes around for the sake of the child as well. But like I told you the other day, you are going to be just fine, emotionally and financially. Simone and I were just discussing your new raise, so we'll be talking to you about that in a few days."

"A raise?" Brooke looked surprised. What we paid her now was competitive, if not more than most executives here in Atlanta. But she deserved every penny of it. She was the best at what she did. I knew she'd received another offer from another company as recently as last week. She assured Simone and me that she wasn't going anywhere.

"Yes, a raise. You deserve it for the way you run this office. It's hard to believe that you graduated from college a year ago. Seriously, Brooke, we are blessed to have you."

"That goes both ways, Dr. Gordon."

Just then, Simone burst though the front doors, surprising both Brooke and me. "Simone, what is going on?" By now, nothing she did should surprise me, but I was curious to see what this was all about.

"Leah, you're not going to believe this." How many times had I heard that over the last few months? As if on cue, the phone rang.

"Well, ladies, I'll leave all the excitement to you. I've got to get back to work," Brooke said as she went to answer the phone.

"Okay, Brooke, we'll see you in a few," I said as Simone grabbed my hand and led me down the hall to my office. Once inside, Simone plopped on the couch, and I took a seat opposite to her. "Okay, what is it?"

"Girl, while I was on my way to work when my friend Lisa called me."

"Who?"

"Lisa Carter. You know, she is a supervisor at one of Bryce's real estate offices. Remember last year we met her at one of the company functions?"

"Okay yes, so she called you and said what?"

"She says they were in a board meeting that Bryce had called, and there was a knock on the door. Lisa was the closest, so she opened the door, and a man walked in, tall, nice looking man. She said he had on a suit as well and looked like he belonged in the meeting with the rest of them, but Lisa says she'd never seen him before. Bryce stood up and addressed the man. Bryce reached his hand out to take the envelope the man was holding. Bryce took the envelope and sat down, but the man stood there for a moment. 'Mr. Gordon, you've been served.' The man turned and left the office as Bryce jumped up screaming, '*What*? Served? For what? Get out! Everybody, just leave *now*!' Lisa said she'd never seen people move so fast as everyone in the room practically ran from the conference room. She said she had to fight for control she wanted to laugh so bad. I wish I could have been there. So, Leah, he's been served. How do you feel about that?"

I was nervous, and I couldn't even pretend to hide that fact. "I don't know, Simone. It makes me a little nervous. I don't know how he's going to react. I mean. getting served during your own board meeting? Can you imagine how embarrassed he is?" We looked at each other for a moment, and then we both burst out laughing. But it wasn't long before I felt the nervousness again. Bryce had been so unpredictable lately. Simone noticed my worried expression and stopped laughing.

"You know you and the kids can come stay with me for a while." I could do just that, and I knew it. But even though I was a little worried, I refused to panic and let Bryce run me away from my home.

"For right now, I'll stick it out at home. But please keep the option open."

"You know I will." Simone looked down at her watch. "It's that time. I have a patient in twenty minutes, so I'll see you for lunch."

"Sounds like a deal."

At quarter after six, we all walked out of the building. Simone and I waved good-bye to Brooke as she headed toward her car. My cell phone rang. I stopped walking when I realized it was Veronica Sanchez. "Hello, Veronica. How are you?"

"I'm fine, I just wanted to touch base with you and let you know that Mr. Gordon was served today." I smiled at Simone. She'd put her things in her car and was waiting on me.

"Yes, I already know." And then I explained to her that Simone's friend worked for Bryce and was there when he was served.

"Okay, just be cautious, and I'll be in touch."

"Okay, I'll talk to you soon. Good night."

I hung up with Veronica, and Simone and I walked over to my car. "So did she say what's next?"

"Well, she'd told me the other day that once he gets served, he gets a chance to respond. She says she's sure she'll hear from his lawyer soon. On Friday we should know when our first court date will be."

"How do you feel about that?"

"Honestly, I feel fine. Ever since the first time I stepped into Veronica's office, I knew I was doing the right thing." I looked at Simone's concerned face. "Don't worry. I am fine." And really I was.

"Okay, well you just let me know if there's anything I can do."

"You know I will. Are you ready to go?"

"I have one errand to run, and then I'll meet you at church."

"Sounds good to me," I told her as I got into my car. Darren and Malaysia had already been picked up by my mother. I would just head on over to the church. I would be a little early, but that was fine. I was sure that Granny was already there. She was always early for Bible study, and regular church services as well. Well, today she was going to have some company.

As I pulled into the parking lot of the church, I didn't see my mother's car, so Granny wouldn't be here early tonight. I knew she was riding with Mama today and wherever they were right now, Granny was probably fussing because she wasn't here already. Looking for a parking space, I spotted Graye's car. There was an empty space right next to it. I was tempted to park there. But I resisted temptation and parked on the other side of the parking lot. I really needed to limit my interaction with him. At any given moment throughout the day, I found myself thinking of him. I'd remember something he said or the way he smiled. A lot of the time I thought of the way he'd prayed for me that one night. I'd felt safe and comforted. I could see the Jesus in him, and it felt genuine and true. And that made things all the more exciting for some reason. I guess it was because I'd never dated or really spent time with a godly man. And now, Graye had me wondering what that was like. Still thinking of him, I got out of the car and turned to walk toward the church and slammed right into someone. Bryce. Nervously, I looked around. There was no one else out here. Where had he come from? I didn't even see his car. And then, before I had a chance to say or do anything at all, Bryce grabbed me around my throat and slammed me against my car. I lost my breath as he began choking me.

I tried to fight him off, but looking into his determined eyes, I began to feel something I'd rarely felt in my lifetime: fear. His eyes were crazed. *Oh, Lord, please don't let me die in the church parking lot.*

"So, you thought you'd have me served during a board meeting. Did you think that was funny?" he yelled into my face. "You won't get anything, I will leave you penniless. I don't think you know who you're messing with. I can get to you and your business." I was starting to feel weak as he continued to choke me. I gathered my strength and fought him with all I had. I hit, slapped, and punched, but to no avail. It was as if he didn't feel any of it.

Air, I need air.

"You are going to pay for this. Divorce me? I don't think so. I'll decide when this marriage is over. I will—"

The next thing I knew, Bryce was lifted up off the ground and his hands were no longer around my neck. Coughing and choking, I struggled to take long, deep breaths. When I finally looked up, Bryce was on the ground and Graye was standing over him. Graye looked at me with concern in his eyes. "Leah, are you okay?" I was still shaking, but I was just glad Graye had shown up. And I was glad to be alive.

"I'll be okay Graye."

I looked at Bryce, who looked from me to Graye, and I could see the hatred in his eyes. "So this is why you filed for divorce," he said as he attempted to get up off the ground. Graye stepped in front of him.

"I seriously suggest you stay on the ground." Looking at Bryce, I could tell he was weighing his options, trying to decide whether or not to take Graye on. In the end, he decided not to get up. But that didn't stop his mouth.

"Hey, you came out of the church. Aren't you the pastor? Why, you're a man of the cloth. You can't seriously do anything to me." Bryce sneered up at Graye. "That wouldn't be too God-like, you know." Graye looked down at him.

"No, I am not the pastor. And yes, I am a man of God, and that is exactly why I haven't done to you what I really wanted to, but I advise you not to keep pushing." A police car pulled into the parking lot. For the next ten minutes, Graye and I filled the officer in on what had happened while Bryce cursed me. I watched as he was handcuffed and led away. He turned back to look at me once.

"It's not over, Leah, not by a long shot." He began cursing again once Graye stepped closer to me and put a protective arm around my shoulder. For a moment, I let the warmth of Graye's strong body comfort me.

"Are you sure you're okay?" I was helpless to stop the tears as they came.

"No, I'm really not, Graye, but I will be," I said, reluctantly pulling away from his warmth.

I felt so safe with him, but there was so sense in me getting too comfortable. I just couldn't with all the drama going on. I didn't need any more confusion. I straightened my clothing and picked up my purse. In all the commotion, I hadn't noticed that it had fallen to the ground. "Thank you so much for helping me. I don't know what would have happened if you hadn't shown up."

"You're welcome. I'm just glad I came out of the church when I did. Do you want me to take you home?" He still looked concerned.

"No, let's just go inside."

"You're staying?"

"Yes, if there was ever a time that I needed Jesus, it is right now. I have a favor to ask of you, Graye."

"Yes, what is it?" I watched as the rest of my family pulled into the parking lot and Simone pulled in right behind them.

"Right now, I just want to go into the church. Despite what just happened, something inside says I am supposed to be here. I don't know, maybe it sounds strange, but it's just a feeling I have. Anyway, for right now, could you please not say anything to Simone, Granny, or my mother? I mean, I'll tell them either later tonight or tomorrow. But if we tell them now, I'll never make it inside the church tonight. First of all, Simone and my mother will be going to see Bryce, if you know what I mean. And Granny, I don't know how she's going to take this. I also don't want to scare the kids."

"I won't say a word for now. But with the way he's acting, you will need to tell your family what's going on, they need to be aware of his behavior. I just want to make sure you're safe." I was so grateful that he'd shown up when he had. And I had to admit, even if only to myself, that I was happy he was concerned about me.

"Thank you Graye, for everything. I will tell them, just not now," I said as everyone walked over to us. We all greeted each other. And as we stood there for a few moments talking, I did my best to act normal. Every time I looked at Simone, I could see the question in her eyes. More than anything, I needed a word from *Him* right now.

Almost two hours later, we were on our way home. I listened to the children talk about what they'd done at church and next weekend's picnic. One of the activities was a basketball game between the youth boys and the deacons in the church, and Darren hadn't been able to stop talking about it. Graye, Simone, and I had put a lot of work into planning this picnic. All the adults and the kids alike were excited. I was looking forward to it as well. There were so many positive things going on now at the church, it really kept me going. Three weeks earlier, Graye had been appointed as the new youth minister. Youth from all over the city had been flocking to the church. Graye brought the Word to the children, but he made it plain and he made it real. He also brought a lot of fun, and that's where Simone and I came in as well. We loved being a part of the youth ministry. Initially, I'd thought of changing ministries because of my attraction to Graye. But I was growing spiritually here in this church and in this ministry.

I loved Pastor Richards and his wife, Carol. Besides, up to this point, Graye and I had kept everything on a friendship level. Simone said you could still see it in our eyes, but I couldn't help that. But so far we were keeping things under control, despite the fact that we always seemed to be thrown together in meetings all the time. Tonight, I'd been glad to have him there. Bryce had lost his mind. Who knew what would have happened if Graye hadn't shown up when he did?

I was also glad that I'd decided to stay at church. As soon as I'd walked in, I'd felt peace. I knew I was meant to be there when the pastor said the title of tonight's lesson. We were starting on a new study book, and the title of the lesson was, "What do you do when you've been attacked unexpectedly?" Graye and I had looked at each other then, smiling. We both knew I was supposed to be here tonight. The message had been powerful, as Pastor Richards broke it down and talked of attacks of all kinds, physical and mental. And as he spoke of God's power and love and protection for His children, I felt once again that He was speaking directly to me. Once Bible study was over, Granny and my mother went to say good night to some friends. I gave Darren the car keys, and he and Malaysia took off running toward the car. "I'll be there in just a minute," I called after them. I watched as Graye walked toward me and felt the familiar excitement I felt whenever he was around.

"Bible study was powerful tonight. I see now why you had that feeling about staying."

"Yes, I knew I was meant to be here. I mean, I'll admit when this craziness happened tonight with Bryce, for a split second I wanted to just get in my car and blaze up out of here quick, fast, and in a hurry. But like I said, something inside said 'stay.' And now I'm glad I did. While I know that I have to be careful with Bryce, God does not mean for me to live in fear. You know, I'll be doing some serious praying tonight. And let me ask you to pray for me as well." He smiled that beautiful captivating smile.

"I always do."

Once home, the kids rushed ahead of me, as always, to get inside the house. When I walked into the house, I could already hear the sound of Darren's video game. I went to his room and stood in the doorway. "Hey, you two, don't forget you have school tomorrow. You can play for a little while, and then it's bedtime.

"Okay, Ma," they chorused. I knew they weren't hungry. They'd eaten dinner at church, so I left them to their game. I wasn't hungry either, even though I hadn't eaten since this afternoon. I decided to go watch a movie. I must have fallen asleep, because when I looked up the movie was over. The house was quiet. I went to Darren's room and saw that he and Malaysia had fallen asleep as well.

Nudging Darren, I told him to get into his bed. I carried Malaysia down the hall to her room. My baby wasn't a baby anymore, and boy did I feel the difference in carrying her. I laid her in the bed and pulled her covers over her. I paused at the doorway. She looked so peaceful sleeping. How was I going to tell her and

Darren that our family really was never going to be the same again? It had been one thing for Bryce and me to tell them that we were separating, but now we were going to get a divorce. And while I still felt that I'd made the best decision for all of us, I still worried about how they were going to take it. Still deep in thought, it took a moment before I realized my cell phone was ringing. Running down the hall, I tried to remember where I'd put it. On the kitchen counter, I finally remembered. I ran into the kitchen and grabbed the phone. "Hello?"

"Leah?"

"Yes? Graye?" *Why is he calling?* I looked up at the clock. It was after ten, and he'd never called me before. Even when we had meetings at church, one of the other members always called.

"Yes, it's Graye. Are you okay?" I could hear the concern in his voice.

"Yes, I'm fine. I mean, at least for tonight I shouldn't have to worry about Bryce because he was arrested."

"That's just it, Leah. I found out he was released. He's not in jail tonight." I should have known the great Bryce Gordon wouldn't be locked down for long. Now I was a little nervous.

"Well, he hasn't come by here, and he hasn't called, so I think I'll be okay," I said, sounding unsure even to my own ears.

"Leah, I … um … can you look out the window?"

"Okay, what is it?" I asked, walking over to my window. Looking out the window, I recognized the familiar Chrysler 300 parked on the side of the curb.

Putting the phone down, I walked out of the house toward Graye's car. I couldn't believe he was here. What was even crazier was the fact that I was excited to see him. The last thing I should be feeling was the thrill I was feeling. I walked around to the driver's side, and Graye, seeing the question in my eyes, held up a hand. "Please, Leah, let me speak first. First, I want to say that I'm not a stalker. It's just that when I found out that Bryce had been released, this feeling came over me. I'm sorry if you feel that I've overstepped my boundaries, but I just had to see for myself that you were okay." His voice was strong and powerful as he gazed at me. "And I won't apologize for wanting to protect you." I stared at him, speechless for a moment. The things that he said and did were so unlike anything I'd ever known. The intense sincerity in his eyes and the fact that he'd actually cared enough to come over here simply blew me away.

"Graye, I don't know what to say except thank you. I ... " my voice trailed off as I tried and failed to find the words to say. He'd taken me by surprise. The truth was, I didn't really want to talk. I wanted to snatch open his door and kiss him.

"You don't have to thank me. I care about you, and I care about Darren and Malaysia. I wanted to do this."

Why? Why does he have to be this perfect? "Well ... um, can I offer you something to drink?"

"No, I'm fine, but thank you for asking."

"Well, the kids are sleeping. I guess I'd better get back inside." *Because if I don't I'm going to kiss you.*

"Good night, Graye." I started to walk away when I heard him call me.

"Leah?" Sighing, I turned around and faced him. I was trying so hard to keep my emotions in check.

"If you don't mind, I'd like to stay out here for a little while."

"But what about Taylor? Where is she?"

"Her Aunt Louise is sick. Taylor has been helping her out this week. She's coming home on Friday. We've got to get ready for the annual church picnic."

"Graye, I really do appreciate your concern, but you don't have to do this."

"I know, but it would just make me feel better tonight knowing you're out of harm's way. I saw him, Leah. Bryce was choking you." Graye looked away then, and I knew the situation had probably reminded him of what had happened to his own sister. My heart went out to him. And despite the fact that he'd already had so much tragedy, he still showed concern for others. "I know that I can't erase the hurt and pain of the situation, but I can make you feel safe. That's what I want, Leah, for you to feel safe."

"Okay," I said, not knowing what else to say. "Good night."

"Good night."

chapter 11

Once I was back inside the house, I stood there leaning against the door. He'd said he cared about me and the children. I remembered the look of honesty in those powerful gray eyes, and I believed him. He wanted to protect me, and boy did I want to be protected by him. This man was stirring up emotions inside, and that really scared me. If I was feeling this way now, how long would it be before I was completely in love with him? And at that point, how would I be able to keep up the pretense of just being his friend? Who was I kidding? I already felt like I was falling for him. And he never pressured me. Ever since the day he'd told me how he felt at Granny's house, he'd never said another word about it again. He didn't have to; I could see it every time I looked into his eyes.

Finally, getting a little bit of an appetite, I decided to eat the chicken Caesar salad I'd picked up earlier. While I sat in the kitchen eating, I thought of what Bryce had done tonight. I had never seen him this out of control. And even though we'd previously fought, tonight there was something different. It was as if he'd been possessed. I shuddered to think of what would have happened if there had been no one there to help me. How far would he have gone?

After finishing my salad, I washed the dish and put it back in the cabinet. Not able to resist, I walked over to the kitchen window to see if Graye was still there. He was. A small glimmer of light bounced off the passenger window. He was reading. Smiling to myself, I pulled the curtain back in place. When he'd asked to stay, I hadn't really known what to say, but now I truly was glad he was here. Something inside said it was okay. Graye had accomplished exactly what he'd wanted—I felt protected and safe.

I woke up at 5:00 a.m. on the dot, as if I'd actually set the alarm. Normally, I slept through the entire night and woke up between six forty-five and seven. But I knew why this morning was different. Graye. I had to know if he was still here. Getting up to put on my robe, I walked over to the window. *He's still here.* I became fully awake then with a pulsating energy. In an effort to calm my nerves, I made my way down the hall to check on the children. I went to each of their rooms, and they were both sound asleep. But I didn't want to have to answer any questions from them this morning once they were up, so I was going to have to ask Graye to leave. Deep down I really didn't want him to leave. I wasn't ready for that fact either. The least I could do was make him a cup of coffee; he would need that on the way home.

As I waited for the coffee to finish brewing, curious thoughts of Graye drifted through my mind. I wondered if he was an early riser in the morning or if he slept late. Did he like a big breakfast, or would a simple muffin and glass of orange juice suffice? Did he—*What am I doing?* It seemed I was always asking myself that same question when it came to Graye. It was none of my business what his everyday habits, likes, and dislikes were. But even as I told myself this, I realized that the more I saw Graye, the more I wanted to know any and everything about him.

Seeing that the coffee was ready, I got a coffee mug from the cabinet and poured him a cup. As the steam and smell of coffee filled the kitchen, I realized I didn't know how he took his coffee. For some reason, I didn't figure him to be a sugar and cream type of man. For now I'd go with my instincts, I could always add the amenities later. I took the steaming cup of coffee and went outside. Once I got to the car, I could see that Graye was sleeping. He'd reclined in his seat and was laying back comfortably. His Bible was still open on his lap He looked incredibly peaceful. I couldn't take my eyes away from his face. He was the most gorgeous man I'd ever seen. And I was learning that he was just as beautiful inside as well. Suddenly, I felt an overwhelming need to touch his face. Tentatively reaching out, I touched his face. Despite the cool morning, he felt warm. His face felt smooth to the touch. I couldn't believe I was doing this. Graye's eyes opened, and once again—as always when he looked at me—I felt myself drowning.

I was busted. I felt like I'd been caught with my hand in the cookie jar. Before I could remove my hand, Graye placed his hand over mine, all the while never breaking eye contact. When I'd decided to touch his face, I'd placed the coffee mug on top of the car. Now I stood there motionless, with one hand on his face and the other just hanging at my side. I was melting from the intensity in his eyes. Oh, I could just eat, sleep, and drink this man. With his free hand, Graye gently pulled my head toward him through the window. He was going to kiss me. Was the earth trembling, or was it just me? Our lips almost touching, I panicked.

Easing myself back out of the window, I smiled and handed Graye his cup of coffee. He smiled at me as he took the steaming cup from my hands. "How did you know I like my coffee black?"

"Just a guess." I wasn't ready for this. If he kissed me now, there was no way I could even pretend to think of him as just a friend. I needed that pretense right now. Something inside told me that everything would change with that one kiss. And what really scared me was the thought of wanting more. I was already falling for him, but I wasn't ready to share the depth of my feelings.

"We're not going to talk about what just happened are we?" He was already learning how to read me.

"Graye, I just can't right now. Okay?"

In my everyday life, I was strong, confident, and assertive. And with Graye, it wasn't as if I didn't feel confident; it was the fact that he stirred emotions and feelings in me that I hadn't known were there. And with Graye, I already knew it would be all or nothing. He wasn't just looking for some fling; he wanted something serious. Deep down, I knew that I felt the same way he did but I wasn't about to act on anything at this point. I wasn't going to rush into anything with anyone. Still, I trusted Graye. My gut instinct said he was a genuinely good, godly man. For a moment, I'd given in to my emotions, and that's why I'd touched his face. But now I was back to reality.

"Okay, I'll accept that for now, but I do have one thing to say."

"What is it?"

"Well, actually, I owe you an apology. I said I wouldn't step over the line, and here I am about to kiss you, I'm sorry."

"There's nothing to apologize for. I actually started this. I acted, and you reacted. Now finish your coffee," I said, hoping he hadn't heard the slight tremor in my voice.

"Yes, ma'am."

"I know I already said it, but I just want to thank you again. You didn't have to do this. In fact, I don't know many men who would do this without expecting something in return."

"There's no need to thank me. I wasn't going to just stand by and let him hurt you. And staying out here tonight, making sure you and the kids are safe, that came from the heart. I wanted to do this. Anytime you need me, Leah, I will be here." Not really knowing how to respond, we both fell silent. I knew he'd heard Bryce when he was screaming about the divorce papers, but he hadn't even mentioned it, and I was grateful for that. He finished his coffee and handed me the mug. "Thank you for the coffee. Well, I know that Darren and Malaysia will be waking up soon, so I'll leave now so you won't have to answer a million questions."

"You're right about that," I said, laughing.

"Okay, so I'll see you later today."

"Later today?" I asked, my mind blank.

"Now, Dr. Gordon, how could you forget that you have a session with Taylor today?"

"Oh yes, I do." I was embarrassed. I couldn't believe I'd forgotten about the session. But when Graye was around, my mind just went completely blank sometimes. "I'm not usually so forgetful."

"I know," he said, looking at me as if he knew exactly why I'd forgotten. "You know she's been talking about that session all week. She really does love you."

"I love her too. There's a joke around the office that she's my third child."

"Maybe one day she will be." My heart began to pound again.

"Graye!" He held up his hands in surrender.

"Okay, okay, I'm sorry for that one. I couldn't resist." He laughed. But I knew he wasn't joking, and deep down his words had caused a tiny twinge of excitement. "Okay, Leah, I'm gone. I'll see you later, and have a good day." Graye flashed me that gorgeous smile as he started his car.

"You too. Bye." I waved as he drove away. Once again, I had the feeling of missing him. *Girl, you have got to get a grip*, I thought to myself.

"My my, aren't we in a good mood today? I see that smile. Okay, now let me guess. Is it the fact that your other daughter is coming in today, or is it the uncle that has you smiling like this?" Simone had breezed into my office, looking absolutely stunning in a red Gucci pants suit. She sat down on the couch with her arms folded across her chest. The look on her face said she was waiting for some answers. My friend didn't miss a beat, and she knew something was up. *Well, I might as well start this story from the beginning,* I thought. I took a deep breath as I prepared myself for the outburst that would surely come once I told Simone what had happened. Glancing at the clock, I realized I had about forty-five minutes before Taylor arrived.

Over the next ten minutes, I told her everything that had happened with Bryce the night before. I watched as her look turned from concern to absolute shock. Even to my own ears, the events of the night before sounded unreal and horrifying. And it had happened to me. "Leah, I just can't get my mind around this. All this happened to you in the last twenty-four hours, and you didn't even tell me at church last night." She jumped up then and began pacing around the office. Her beautiful, exotic eyes danced with angry fire. "If I could just get my hands on Bryce Gordon right now."

"See, that's exactly why I didn't tell you last night. You and my mother would have hunted Bryce down to the ends of the earth."

"You're right about that. I can't believe he put his hands on you."

"You and me both."

Taking a deep breath, Simone sat down again and stared at me for a moment. I watched as conflicting emotions moved across her face. She wanted to say something. "What is it, Simone?"

"What happened to you reminds me of another night." Now it was my turn to look concerned. I moved from my desk to the other end of the couch where she was sitting.

"What night, Simone? What are you talking about?" I didn't know what, but I figured the who. She had to be talking about Chris. She was finally going to tell me what had really happened between them. Over the years, she'd given me bits and pieces here and there, but I'd always known there was more. The relationship had surely been catastrophic, but I knew there was something she hadn't told me. I'd always felt that when she was ready, she would.

When I fell for Chris, I fell hard. Hard and fast. And it was so different. In the beginning, everything was so perfect. He was romantic, understanding, and funny. Just everything a woman would want in a man. The only problem was that I couldn't get him to go to church with me. It wasn't a big deal. I mean, I just figured in time he'd come around.

"Anyway after that first year we had a real big blowout because I wanted to go to Virginia for the annual church retreat. Well, he didn't want to go, and he didn't want me to go either. I couldn't understand what the big deal was; it was for one weekend. But more importantly, I found myself justifying my actions with him, something I had never done with a man before. So I gave him a piece of my mind, like I'd done all my life when people made me mad. Then I left the apartment. I must have driven around for hours. And when I was ready to, I headed home." Simone stopped for a moment. She took a deep breath, as if gathering courage to continue. This was hard for her, I could tell. Wanting her to know that I was here for her without actually speaking, I reached over and squeezed her hand lightly. She smiled at me, letting me know she was okay.

"I never saw it coming, Leah. I walked into the front door, and I just can't describe how I felt when Chris walked over to me and punched me in the face. The next thing I knew, I was falling. For a moment, I sat there on the ground, staring up at him in shock. You know we watch these movies where woman get beat, and we yell and scream at the television, telling them what to do. We say what we would do if we were that woman. But you know, when it happens to you, it becomes different. It becomes so real. And I'm sure that there are women out there who do jump right up and fight like there's no tomorrow. But there are those of us who just go into shock. I mean, this just didn't happen to me. But even as I felt my anger rise, I couldn't move, I couldn't speak.

"And then he began to kick me. I tried to get away, but I couldn't. His kicks were hard, fast, and painful. Chris continued to kick me until I lost the will, the power, to even try to move." Simone stopped and stood up then. She walked over to the window, and when she faced me again, her beautiful face was the portrait of sadness. We were both crying now, and my heart went out to my friend. Even though I hadn't actually been there with her, I could actually feel physical pain. Her voice shook with emotion as she spoke now. "He broke me that night, Leah. He broke me in ways I'd never been broken. And when he was done kicking me, he smiled as he leaned over and whispered in my ear, 'I'll never let you leave me alive.' I lay there on the ground, and I let fear take over. He stood up then looked down at me for a moment. 'Don't even think you're going to the hospital. I know someone who's going to fix you right up.' When he said that, I wanted to jump up and just get out of there, but I couldn't move. Unspeakable pain had my entire body throbbing.

"About thirty minutes later, there was a knock on the door, and the street doctor walked in. I recognized him right away, because some of the women in my own family had called him when one of their men had gotten out of hand. His real name was Travis, and when people got hurt and didn't want anyone to know about it, they called him. I felt humiliation wash over me, as I knew he recognized me as well. His voice shook when he told Chris my family wasn't going to like this. Chris grabbed Travis by the arm and began to twist it. 'That's why no one is going to know about this accept for the people in this room.

I could tell he didn't want to, but Travis finally agreed to keep quiet. So this humiliation continued for about ten minutes as Travis opened my shirt to check me over for broken bones. I could see the pity in his eyes as he looked at me. Even though he touched my skin lightly, the pain was almost unbearable. I wanted to scream and knock his hand away. But I was powerless. With even the slightest hint of movement my, body convulsed in complete and utter agony. Travis found that I didn't have any broken bones, luckily, so all he needed to do was bandage me around the waist to limit my movement and give me something for the pain. As Travis moved to pick me up off the ground, Chris moved in front of him. 'I'll take care of this part. No one carries my woman into our bedroom but me.' I could only whimper as Chris picked me up roughly from the floor. He looked down at me, smiled, and said, 'Suck it up. It can't hurt that bad.' Travis tried to come to my defense and tell Chris I was in a lot of pain, but Chris silenced Travis with a single look as he practically dumped me on the bed.

"Under Chris's watchful eye, Travis bandaged me up and gave me a shot of morphine. Once he packed up his medical supply bag, he walked toward the door to the bedroom. He turned around and looked at me one last time. In his eyes I could see his question. Shaking my head no, I stared back at him until I knew he understood. Travis left silently, and I knew my secret was safe with him. The next day, Chris showered me with flowers and gifts and acted as if nothing had happened. When I didn't show any enthusiasm for the new diamond earrings, he threw the flowers in my face. He knew he had the power now. The balance of our relationship was forever changed. I'd let fear take over, and now he was in control." Simone stood up and began to pace again. "I was so humiliated. So ashamed."

Simone stopped then and faced me. "So many times over the months that followed, I wanted to tell you what was going on. I would never tell my family, but I came close to telling you. I guess I just had this fear that you would think less of me as a person. The only thing that really kept me going was what you and I were doing to get our own practice. At the time, I was scared of what he might do, so I kept my dream hidden from him. All he knew was that I was going to work. And he wanted me to work, so he never really questioned me on that. I was able to plan my meetings with you around my workday. And I kept my dream hidden from him. And the more progress you and I made, the more my confidence began to build again. And I became less and less afraid of him. That next year, when I finally decided I'd had enough, I mapped out my plan to leave him very well. Well, actually, I believe the Lord intervened on my behalf, because Chris's job called one night with an emergency assignment; he had to fly to Chicago immediately.

"For two weeks, he was going to be gone. Two weeks! I couldn't believe it. God had answered my prayers. It took everything in me not to jump out of that bed shouting for joy as Chris stared at me. He was furious, and I could tell. He didn't want to leave me, but he had no choice. And he couldn't take me with him because another colleague was going to be joining him. As if he could hear the wheels spinning in my head, he yanked me across the bed until I was practically in his lap. Then complete silence as we sat there facing each other, eye to eye. After months and months of pretending, I had become very good at hiding my true feelings. I let nothing show as he continued to stare me down. I knew he was testing me, trying his best to figure out what I was thinking. The next morning, he hit me a couple of times to make sure I knew who was still in charge. 'Don't even think about doing anything while I'm gone. You know if you leave, I will find you. And it won't be pretty.' And then he was gone.

"I put those two weeks to good use. Girl, I—" We both paused as Brooke beeped in on my line.

"Dr. Gordon, you have a delivery, and Taylor will be here in about ten minutes." I stood up to prepare for my session with Taylor.

"Simone, I am so sorry. You know we have got to continue this later." She walked over to me, and we hugged.

"Yes, we will continue this later, because you are treating me to dinner."

"That sounds like a plan."

"Okay, now let's go see what Graye sent you."

"How do you know it's from Graye?" I asked her as we walked out of my office. Simone didn't answer but just gave me a look as we walked over to Brooke, who was all smiles. There sitting on the counter was a beautifully made chocolate bouquet. It had every kind of chocolate you could think of, and it all came together in the shape of a heart.

My heart beat a mile a minute as I looked at the card. It was from Graye, and it read, "I know this is going to sound strange, but this gift isn't really about trying to sweep you off your feet. You are beautiful, and every time I look at you, you take my breath away. And I'd be lying if I didn't admit that on some level I do want to impress you. But this is about me genuinely caring for the woman in you. It's about rebuilding what another man tried to tear down. I care, and I'm thinking of you." Closing my eyes, his words swirled around in my head until they settled and found life in my heart and mind. And I was warmed at the thought of him thinking of me. I couldn't even stop the smile that seemed to have a life of its own as it spread across my face.

Becoming aware that Simone and Brooke were staring at me, I attempted to pull myself together. "Okay, Brooke, can you keep this up front for me right now. I don't want it to distract me from my session with Taylor."

"Oh, don't go trying to get all professional on us now. We saw the way you just lit up, didn't we, Brooke?" I looked at Brooke for help, but she was smiling and shaking her head at me.

"I have to admit, Dr. Gordon, I haven't seen you smile like that before."

"Oh no, not you too, Brooke. I'm going to my office now," I said as they both erupted in laughter.

"Run now, but we'll talk about this at dinner," Simone warned as she went to her own office. I looked at my bouquet once more; it really was lovely. Taking the bouquet with me, I smiled all the way back to my office.

chapter 12

At the end of our session, I stood up to see Taylor out. I didn't do it with anyone else; it had just become a habit with Taylor. "Dr. Leah, can I ask you something?"

"Sure, Taylor, what is it?"

"How do you feel about my uncle Graye?" Completely caught off guard, I just stood there for a moment, not sure what to say. Taylor, serious now waited expectantly for my answer.

"Well ... um, Taylor, I think your uncle is a very nice man." That sounded weak even to me. She stood there watching me for a moment. I could tell she wanted to say something but wasn't quite sure how to say it.

"Well, he doesn't say anything to me but whenever your name comes up, he just smiles and lights up. I think he likes you."

"I like him too, as a friend." She wasn't making this easy for me. Just then, Brooke beeped in.

"Dr. Gordon, your eleven o'clock just called and said she'll be five minutes late if that's okay."

Talk about being saved by the bell. "Come on, Taylor. Let me see you out." I loved her to death, but she was asking me things I didn't even want to admit to myself. As I walked Taylor to the door, I could see Graye's car outside. I forced myself to act normal as I walked outside and approached the car with Taylor. I had had just seen him this morning, but that didn't stop the electrifying ripples I was feeling inside.

"Hello, Leah."

That voice, that man. "Hello, Graye. How are you?" He had watched over me all night, and he didn't look in the least bit tired. He looked absolutely delectable. *Stop it, Leah.* I couldn't help it, though. He always had this effect on me whenever he was around. I wondered if I had the same effect on him. We spoke volumes with our eyes. *Those eyes.*

Taylor, who had been standing there taking everything in, began to giggle. Children were just too smart for their own good. "Okay, Taylor, say good-bye to Dr. Leah and get in the car." She hugged me as she shook her head, smiling, and hopped into the car. It took me a moment to realize I was still standing there smiling like some teenager. "Well, I'll see you later."

"Okay, see you later. Graye?"

"Yes?"

"Thank you, for *everything.*"

"You are most welcome, Leah."

I stood there watching as he drove away. Unexpectedly, I felt a flutter of sadness watching him leave. Turning to go back inside, I could see Simone standing at the door, holding it open for me. Even in the distance, I could see the smile on her face. *Great.* I wondered how much she'd seen. "Thank you," I said, attempting to pass through and ignoring the look on my friend's face.

"Oh yes, dinner is going to be very interesting tonight. Make sure you get a sitter." She playfully swatted me as she went to her own office.

"Okay, so what's up with you and the most beautiful man in the world?" We were sitting in Pinellos, waiting for our food. Looking around the room, I saw couples and families laughing, having a good time. I'd always liked it here. The restaurant was elegant without the stuffiness, and the atmosphere was always relaxed and energized at the same time. The combination had made it one of our favorite places to come to. Putting on a serious expression, I looked at Simone. I wanted to hear the rest of the story about Chris, since we'd been interrupted earlier. I knew she had changed offices at her old practice and had moved across town, but at the time, she had told me she was transferred. It seemed like a blessing in disguise because she and Chris were having relationship problems. Now I understood the real reason for these drastic changes.

"Okay, but before we get into that, finish telling me about how you left Chris."

"Well, he left for two weeks. I moved across town to a new apartment. My practice had opened up a new office, so I changed offices. I knew he'd go to my old office, but he wasn't able to find out anything because personal information isn't given out. Basically, I disappeared, and in the process I got myself a restraining order. If there was one thing that I knew about Chris, it was that he did not want to go to jail. It took some time, but I healed from the situation." She patted my hand from across the table. "You don't have to worry about me, I am fine." I smiled at her reassuringly.

"I know. I just wish you would have told me, I could have been there for you."

"It was me, Leah. I know I could've trusted you. I was just so ashamed. But whether you know it or not, you were there for me. With our focus on opening our own office, it gave me strength and determination to fight for our dream and get rid of anything that would hinder that dream. I got rid of him, and we did it. Now, I want to get back to a much more interesting topic."

"Simone, I don't even know where to start."

"Start from the beginning."

"Well, after Bryce went to jail, I went home with the kids. Graye called me and told me that Bryce had gotten out of jail. I am telling you, when I heard that, I have to admit, it scared me a little. He'd been so out of control. I didn't know what he was capable of. But I didn't need to worry." I smiled for a moment before continuing.

"Okay, what's up? Why didn't you have to worry?" I looked at my friend sitting there with anticipation on her face. She was going to love this.

"Well, while I was talking to Graye, he told me to look outside my window. So guess what I saw when I looked out the window?"

"Leah, if you don't stop it and tell me—"

"Okay, okay, it was Graye; he was outside."

"What?"

"Yes, I could hardly believe it myself as I walked outside to his car." Simone was sitting on the edge of her seat now. Both of us barely took notice as the waitress placed our entrees on the table. She'd ordered the baby-back ribs, and I had the shrimp scampi. "So what did he say? Why was he there?"

"To watch over me. He said he was concerned for me and the children, and he wanted to make sure we were okay."

"Oh, see, I knew I liked Graye Barrington. That has got to be the sweetest thing."

"There's more."

"More?" I laughed at her expression. She was really into this. "Yes, he actually asked me if it was okay if he stayed the night." Simone's eyebrows raised in question. "No, not that kind of stay the night. He wanted to stay in his car and just watch over the house for me."

"Oh, you have got to be kidding me. They don't make men like that anymore. Are you telling me that this man stayed outside all night and just watched over the house? He didn't try to come in at least once?"

"No, he didn't. I woke up this morning, and he was still there. I made him some coffee, and when I went outside, he was sleeping. And I'll be honest, Simone, when I saw him there sleeping peacefully with his Bible across his lap, I felt something for him."

"Honestly, you've always felt something for him."

"Okay, you're right, but this morning sealed the deal, so to speak."

"Graye Barringtion is a man after my own heart, and yours too apparently. So what are you going to do?"

"Do?"

"Yes, this man has in so many words let you know how he feels, so what are you going to do about what you feel?" she asked, taking a bite of one of her ribs.

"I'm not going to do anything right now. I'm in the middle of a divorce. And then I have to think of the kids right now."

"Excuses, excuses. Those kids already like Graye, especially Darren. You can tell he looks up to him."

"I know. I'm just still sorting through everything. I'm not ready for this yet, and I don't know when I will be."

"But he's getting in here, isn't he?" Simone asked, pointing to her heart. Graye's face and the sincerity in his eyes flashed across my mind as I answered her.

"Yes, Simone, he really is."

Two days later, the kids ran excitedly through the house. I'd finally given in and decided to let them go to Granny's for the summer. They wouldn't be that far away, and I'd still see them all the time. Plus, I knew that if they were with her, I wouldn't have to worry at all. They were also ecstatic because of the picnic. Today was the big day, and Darren couldn't wait to get there and play in the basketball game. Malaysia was one of the cheerleaders, and she just couldn't wait to get to her friends. I was looking forward to the picnic as well. We'd picked Rosedale Park. There would be good food, gospel music, and all different types of activities that catered to the young as well as the older generations. As we stepped outside, the kids ran to the car with their bags. We were going to meet Granny there, and when the picnic was over, they would leave with her and my mother. Humming to myself as I walked to the car, I waved to my next-door neighbor. I looked around, taking in the slight breeze. The sun was shining, with not one cloud in the sky. Today was going to be a good day.

When we arrived at the picnic, the kids practically hopped out of the car. They barely said good-bye as they both took off in different directions. Getting out of the car, I stood for a moment, taking everything in. It was an absolutely beautiful today, and the picnic was in full swing. A lot of members had shown up, and not by themselves either. There were new faces, as members had brought family and friends alike. It looked as though everyone was having a good time. Hearing my name called, I turned to my right to see my mother and Granny waving frantically at me. I smiled as I waved back and headed toward them. When I was a few feet away from them, a figure stepped in from the side. Graye. I had seen him a lot the last few days, and yet every time was like the first time. This man was seriously having an effect on me. Wanting to appear normal, I approached the group with what I hoped did not look like a nervous smile. As I spoke, I could feel the intensity of Graye's eyes on me. I struggled and fought the urge to turn to him.

I listened as Granny talked about the success of the picnic. *Stop it, Graye.* He was still staring; I could feel it. But I didn't really want him to stop, even though he was making me so nervous I could barely concentrate on the conversation. As everyone talked for a few more minutes, I thought of how I would escape. Spotting Rain sitting at a nearby table, I waved. She waved back and motioned me over. Perfect, I had my escape. "Hey, everybody, I'm going to talk to Rain, I'll see you soon." I couldn't resist looking at Graye as I walked away. He tried to hide the look of disappointment on his face with a smile, but those eyes said it all—so deep and truthful. I couldn't help shivering slightly as I saw everything in his eyes.

Mentally pulling myself away, I turned and smiled as I walked over to Rain. I sat down across from her. We caught glimpses of each other at church, but we hadn't really gotten together. Still the transformation in her was evident. She'd even been chosen as the new director of the children's ministry. Gone was the gossip and troublemaker. She was occupying her time with the children in the church, and she was doing a great job. "Girl, we have been playing some serious phone tag."

"I know, and it's my fault. I have been so busy with the kids' ministry. I keep saying I need to call you, and then something else happens."

"Well, I know how it can be. And I've been meaning to tell you, you are doing a wonderful job with the children's ministry."

"Thank you, and so are you with the youth ministry. I guess we both found our callings."

"Yes, we did," I said, smiling. The youth ministry really was a blessing to me. Rain looked away, and when she turned back to me, there was a seriousness in her face.

"Rain, what's up?"

"I wanted to apologize to you."

"What are you apologizing for? I know you've been busy. I can understand that."

"No, it's not about that. It's something I should have apologized to you for a long time ago. When we were kids, I wasn't very nice to you. Well, I wasn't really nice to anyone, but I remember being especially hard on you."

"Rain, it's okay. That was so long ago. And we were just teenagers then." I patted her hand as I gave her a reassuring smile. She smiled as well, but there was still a seriousness there, lingering beneath the surface.

"Leah, I want to share something with you that I've never really shared with anyone." I leaned forward and listened intently as Rain told a story of heartache and pain.

"My house was the quiet house, at least that's what I always called it. My parents were Clarence and Virginia Howard. I also had two younger brothers, but it was always as if I were alone, a stranger in my own home. Even as a toddler, I could feel the coldness, although then, I didn't quite know what to call it. My parents worshiped the boys, showered them with love and affection, and to my father, my brothers could do no wrong. But I was treated as an outsider. It wasn't that he beat me or anything. Even when I misbehaved, my father wouldn't touch me or even say a word. He would look at my mother first, as if to say I told you so, but there was a real meanness to it. And she would always look back at him with an apology in her eyes. Many times, she would start to cry and run from the room. Even her cries were silent.

"My mother was a beautiful, lonely person. Her skin was a beautiful, golden-brown and smooth as silk. She was a small, petite woman with stunning deep, brown eyes and hair so long it simply flowed down her back. I didn't look anything like her. Where she was small and petite, I was tall and very thin. The only physical thing we had in common was our long, thick hair, and because of that, my hair was something I always cherished. Childishly, I thought the prettier I did my hair, mother would notice me, love me. I just wanted so badly to be close to my mother, but she wouldn't let me. Growing up, I never understood why. It wasn't really anything she said, but if I tried to be loving or get some kind of affection from her, she would look at me with those big sad eyes, and right before my eyes, she would withdraw from me. It hurt so much. The rejection from my mother was almost too much to bear at times because even as she rejected me, my love for her only seemed to grow. If she showed me any kind of attention at all, I noticed my father would punish her, but silently. And then she'd withdraw from me even more.

"I remember when I was ten years old, I was walking down the hallway one day, and my parents' bedroom door was slightly open. I could see mother sitting in front of the mirror. She was brushing her hair and humming. I had no idea what song she was humming. Just the fact that she was happily humming was a joyous sight to see. I walked over to the door and opened it. In the mirror, I saw her look at me, and still she continued to hum and brush. I took this as a sign of encouragement as I entered her room. My excitement grew as I approached her, and she didn't run away from me as if I were a plague. As she hummed, I gently took the brush from her and began to brush her hair. I watched as tears ran down her cheeks, but she didn't stop me; she continued to hum. For the very first time, I felt a connection as I began to hum along with her. I felt as if I would burst with pure happiness. Mother and daughter together, humming a song and just being girls. It was something I'm sure thousands, no millions, of mothers and daughters did every day. But this was new to me. It was precious and beautiful. And it lasted all of three minutes.

"I could hear him even before he entered the room. My father's loud footsteps echoed as he rushed down the hallway and entered the room. Instantly, my mother stopped humming as we turned and faced him. In one swift movement, my father snatched the brush out of my hand and threw it against the wall. We all stood there then, my father staring at my mother with accusing eyes, and she stared back at him, once again with an apology in her eyes. And I knew I had lost my mother. After that, she sank into a depression that she never came out of. Just a few months later, she was gone. She packed up her things, and that was it; we never saw her again. She left a note for my father, but he never let us see it. I assume she left because of me. I was angry and hurt. I would see you and other girls laughing and enjoying life. And me, I just had this gaping hole inside, and there was no one to turn to, nowhere to go. I hated it, and with my mother gone, the silence in the home seemed to reach out and engulf me even more.

"My father turned to my brothers for comfort and they turned to him, but for me, there was no one. In my anger, I went to school and caused trouble. I talked, yelled, and lied about any and everything. Anything to get attention, I would do. And still my father ignored me. I even caused trouble in church, thinking that would *make* him notice me. Still nothing. Surprisingly, though, my grades in school were always really good. If there was one thing I wanted to do more than cause my usual trouble, it was to get away from my father. At eighteen, I was at the top of my class, and I received a four-year scholarship to Spelman. I remember it was a week before I was to leave school, and I was walking through the neighborhood. I looked up, and that's when I saw one of my mother's old friends motioning for me to come over to her. My mother didn't talk to a lot of people, but Ms. Ann had been a friend of my parents' since childhood. I walked over to her. She asked me to come sit with her for a while. Not having anything better to do, I walked up the steps to join her on the porch. I sat in a chair across from her. 'So tell tell me, Rain, why do you always look so angry?'

"A thousand responses came to mind as I looked into Ms. Ann's kind face. She couldn't possibly understand the things I went through. I was now eighteen years old and mad with the world. Out of the blue, she just said it was time she told me a story. She said she could see pain written all over my face and that this story would make a difference in my life. Ms. Ann leaned across the open space separating us and touched my face softly. Not used to any kind of affection, I jumped out of her reach. I looked away from her sad, knowing eyes. 'Yes, damage has already been done. It's time you know the truth, and that daddy of yours is never going to tell you.' The suspense was killing me. I asked her to just tell me the story, but she told me there was something I needed to see and hurried into the house.

"I didn't have long to wait, because about a minute later she was back. She walked over to me and placed an old photo album in my lap. 'Look through those first, and then we'll talk,' she told me.

For the next ten minutes, I was transformed as I was taken back to a time where my mother was young and beautiful and happy. She leaped out at me from the pages. I couldn't stop the tears as they flowed. This was my mother in another life, a happier life. She smiled in almost every picture, her lovely hair framing her face. There were all kinds of pictures with my mother, Ms. Ann, my father, and another young man who looked familiar. 'Who is this, Ms. Ann,' I asked, pointing to the young man in the photos. I could see Ms. Ann's hesitation. She told me his name was Mark Davion. She said she wanted me to enjoy the rest of the pictures and she would tell me about him in a minute. Then she told me that when my mom was pregnant with me, she had wanted me to have it. I couldn't believe it. This was mine. As I turned the pages, the book took on even more meaning as I realized this was a gift from my mother. And it meant something—at some point she'd thought about me, cared about me. I laughed to myself as I looked at her various poses for the camera.

My father and the other young man joined my mother in most of the pictures.

The last picture in the album showed this Mark Davion playing basketball. My mother stood watching him from the sidelines. The person taking the picture had really focused in on mother's face as she gazed at Mark. The look was intense; it was passionate. I felt butterflies as I instinctively realized my mother had been in love with this man. The picture said it all, yet I felt there was more. I closed the book and held it to me. Looking up at Ms. Ann, I tried to prepare myself as the butterflies continued their dance inside of me. Ms. Ann settled back in her seat as she began to tell me a story I'd never heard and would never have even imagined to be true."

chapter 13

"'When we were all young in school, they used to call your mother, Clarence, and Mark the triple threat. They were always together. I hung out with them too, but it was those three that were inseparable. As they got older, it was clear to see that your daddy thought of your mother as more than a friend. But it was Mark who had your mother's heart. And Mark was just as in love with her as she was with him. Once Clarence caught them kissing, and from the look on his face, you would've thought someone had actually took out a gun and shot him. By then we were all teenagers, hormones raging and all that. The day he saw your mother and Mark kissing changed everything forever. After that, Clarence treated Mark as his rival. Mark played basketball and football like he was born for it. He even had the top grades in high school. He was just naturally good at everything. He was one of those people you watched in life that made everything seem effortless yet so beautiful; it was like watching art in motion. All the girls were in love with him, but he only had eyes for your mother.

"'Well, Clarence wasn't gifted naturally the way that Mark was, but it wasn't for his lack of trying. He challenged Mark at everything, and I mean he made it known he was out to get Mark anyway he could. And as time went on, these two boys who'd been best friends since childhood couldn't stand to be in the same room with each other. Your mother tried to bridge the distance between the two, but for her to truly have been able to do that, she would have had to give up Mark. And if you just watched the two of them together, you just knew that wasn't going to happen.

"'After a while, Mark let his animosity go. I mean he had your mother, and between her, his grades, basketball, and football, his future looked very bright. Well, Clarence didn't have Virginia. His grades were only average, and although he tried his hand at sports, he always seemed to come in second best to Mark. It only made him dislike Mark even more. It was as if he'd started to blame Mark for everything in his life that didn't go right. Yes, ma'am, that situation got very deep," Ms. Ann, said slapping her thigh in confirmation.

"'After high school, Virginia and Mark got engaged. Mark had gotten a full scholarship to play football at the University of Florida. Your mother knew where Mark wanted to go, and she'd applied for Florida herself and had been accepted too. They were so happy, and their happiness was contagious; they just made everyone around them happy as well. Well, Clarence couldn't stand it. Immediately after high school, he enlisted in the army and he was gone.

"'That summer was a summer of plans as Virginia and Mark planned to get married right before going off to college. All the older adults tried to persuade the two to wait, but Mark wasn't hearing any of that. He wanted to marry Virginia, and nothing was going to stop him. Eventually everyone came around, and then the only issue was who was going to pay for the wedding. You probably don't know this, but your mother came from money and was the apple of her father's eye. Mark's family wanted to pay for everything too. In the end they compromised as the wedding plans were made. A week before the wedding, and two weeks before the two were to go off to college together, Mark and his friends went out to party one last time. On the way home, Mark was hit head on by a semi truck and was killed instantly. When Virginia was told, the light went out of her. From that day on, she was never the same.' Before Ms. Ann could finish the story, I heard my father shouting my name, and his voice seemed to be getting closer. 'Not now!' I screamed inside. But I knew I had to answer him or there would be trouble.

"Ms. Anne stopped then and looked into my eyes. For a moment, neither of us moved. 'Go, Rain. I don't want to cause trouble with you and Clarence. I will be here when you're ready for the rest of the story.' I was frustrated as I stood up to go home. Apparently I wasn't fast enough for my father, because a moment later he was there standing in the street right in front of Ms. Ann's house. I stood my ground and told her I wanted to hear the rest of the story. 'I know you do, but it seems as if it isn't the time now,' she said, never taking her eyes from my father. He never said a word to her, but it was as if they were having a silent standoff. 'Rain, I said let's go,' he demanded. She patted my hand as she moved toward her front door. She turned and smiled sadly as she looked at me. 'Don't worry, Rain; I will be here.' Normally just the sight of him would put fear in my heart, but I knew she'd been about to tell me something important, so I was torn between the need to hear my mother's story and fear of another battle with my father. 'Go on, child. Don't get yourself in trouble.' And with that, Ms. Ann disappeared inside her house, taking the mystery and all the questions I still had with her. Reluctantly, I turned and walked home with my father. Before I'd left I'd tried to get back to Ms. Ann's, but my daddy wouldn't let me out of his sight. He insisted on knowing where I was every minute of the day. It was like he knew I was on the verge of uncovering something and he just had to stop me. He even insisted I leave earlier than we'd originally planned, and right before I left, we really had it out. I went to college this insecure, troubled young lady, unsure of the future and all that if held. I think of her all the time, you know. I wonder where my mother is. Why did she leave? Did she really hate me that much?"

Rain stopped talking, and we both sat there in silence for a while. I struggled to absorb this sad story. Looking at Rain, I could tell that while she still didn't have the answers to this mystery, she was experiencing some relief at having shared this with someone. She'd needed me to listen, and I was glad I had. I thought of how I'd judged her, never really knowing why she did the things she did. And I realized that's what we do as people all the time. We judge people who do things that are different or wrong in our eyes, and we condemn them, when all we really have the right to do is pray for them. I smiled at Rain gently as I took hold of her hand from across the table. "I apologize for not looking beneath the surface. I wasn't there then, but I am now. Is there anything I can do?"

"Leah, ever since that sermon Pastor Richards preached where we all ran the race, I have been doing so much better. I feel I have a long way to go, but for the first time, I have hope." Getting up from the table, I walked around and gave her a long hug.

Hearing some commotion, we looked over and saw that a volleyball game was about to take place. We smiled at each other as we thought back to high school. We jumped up at the same time and hugged each other again as we walked over to join the game. At the same time, Graye fell in beside us. "Hey, I think I'll join you."

"Great," we both said, and like a million times before, the butterflies began as they did every time I heard his voice or he was near.

"Oh, good, here are Rain, Graye, and Leah. I've got Leah and Graye," Pastor Graysdon announced. He playfully clapped me on the back. "You two came at the right time."

"Okay, everyone, positions please. Let's get it started," Pastor Graysdon said as he clapped his hands together in anticipation.

"Thank you, Leah. I'll see you later," Rain said as she crossed over to join her team on the other side. All too aware of Graye's presence, I prepared for the game. It was going to be interesting to see if I still had skillz, as Darren would say.

For the next thirty minutes, I let everything go as I played the sport I'd loved as a teenager. As I moved, ran, jumped, and hit the ball, I could feel the adrenaline pumping throughout my body. I hadn't realized how much I missed this. I'd been on the volleyball team in high school, but I'd had to quit once I got pregnant. So I was truly enjoying this today. Throughout the game, I found myself teamed up with Graye. He would set it up, and I would go in for the kill or vice versa. It wasn't long before people started calling us the dynamic duo.

Graye grinned at me as we won another round. Just then, Darren came running over. "Calling all men in the youth versus deacons basketball game. It's time for warm-up." Rain and I laughed as most of the men began to leave the volleyball game. Graye turned toward me as he headed off.

"See you later, Leah. I had fun playing with you. Remember, we are the dynamic duo." And then he was gone, leaving me to feel embarrassed all by myself. I looked over at Rain, who was grinning at me.

"I'm not saying a word, Leah." I grinned back at her as we headed toward the recreation building where the game was being held.

Two ladies I hadn't seen before passed by us, and one looked back at me disapprovingly. She turned to her friend and spoke loud enough so that Rain and I heard their conversation. "Is her divorce even final yet?"

"And did you see the way they were carrying on? This is still a church function."

Instantly, I became angry. How dare they judge me? And how did they even know about the divorce? Rain, seeing my face, stopped me to give me a moment to cool off. "Leah, don't pay any attention to them. It's only jealousy, because they've both been after Graye since he came back and he won't give them the time of day. You could go and confront them, and I'd back you up one hundred percent. But I'd say the best thing you could do for them is pray for them." The old Rain would have egged the entire thing on until something happened, but this was the new Rain, and I was thankful for her.

"Thank you for that. I needed a voice of reason."

"Girl, there are times when we all do."

"Hey, ladies," Simone called, walking over to us. I was glad to see that Adrian was with her. It was about time she gave him a chance. And I could tell by the look on his face he was glad as well. Smiling at Adrian, I made the introductions all around. "Okay, now that I am officially fashionably late, let's find the best seats in the house," Simone said, linking arms with Adrian. We all laughed as we entered the center for the park.

Once inside, we looked around for good seats. It looked as if everyone was trying to find a seat. Seeing the Roberson twins, I waved at them. "Hey, Leah," they called, waving back.

"Hey, I found some seats." Rain, Simone, and I followed Adrian to a middle row of empty seats. Sitting down, I could see Adrian had picked good seats; we would be able to see everything from here. I couldn't wait to see Darren play. Smiling secretly, I admitted to myself that I was also looking forward to seeing Graye play. And as if on cue, he came running out from the back. Both teams followed.

The young men in the youth group came out bursting with energy. I laughed when I saw Darren. "Look at my godson." Simone nudged me. The young men were wearing black jerseys with gold writing on them and black jersey shorts. Their shirts read, "J-Unit," which stood for Jesus Unit. The deacons were dressed similarly, except their jerseys were gold with black writing. Their jerseys read, "ODS," which stood for Original Deacons. We watched as they all threw some practice shots. The deacons were really working hard to get the crowd involved. Darren and his friends were dunking and showing off for the crowd as well. They were so hyped up, and I could tell just by looking at the expressions on their face that they just knew they were going to win. I was getting excited, and the game hadn't even started yet.

Pastor Richards stepped onto the floor, and everyone began cheering. He was dressed like an official referee, and it was hilarious. He waved to the crowd and blew his whistle. Looking around, it was clear to see the basketball game was the main event of the day. The number of people had tripled. Both teams stopped practicing and got ready to play. As Graye ran over to his side, he looked over at me and smiled. Before I knew it, I was smiling back. "Girl, look at that smile." Mentally pulling myself away from that smile, I snapped out of it and attempted to give Simone a warning look.

"Simone he smiles at everyone. He's a nice man."

"Yeah, but he only smiles like that with you." I looked at Adrian for help, but all he did was shake his head as he laughed at the two of us.

For the next hour, we all watched as both teams gave the game their all. And while there was a competitiveness in the air, both teams were genuinely having a good time. During the short halftime show, I couldn't help smiling at Malaysia and her little friends as they performed their cheers. My baby looked absolutely adorable in her cheerleading outfit. "Look at Laysia. She looks so cute," said Simone.

After the show, the game was back in session. Both teams ran up and down the court in determination. It was as if the deacons had decided during halftime that they weren't going out without a fight. A couple of them were really struggling, and it was my guess they hadn't played basketball in years. It was obvious that Graye and Pastor Graysdon were the Michael Jordans of the team. But seeing my son shoot and score points was what really made my heart swell with pride. He almost looked like a man out there. Every time he scored, we all slapped hands and cheered like this was the NBA.

The last five minutes was a frenzy of noise and activity, as both teams were tied. Both teams had given all they had. People shouted and cheered for the team they wanted to win. "So which team do you want to win, Leah? Divided loyalties," Simone said. I could hear the laughter in her voice.

Rain laughed and looked at me. "Is she always like this?"

"Always," Adrian and I responded at the same time. I shot Simone another warning look, which didn't seem to be working in the least. I turned my attention back to the court. I was determined not to let her make me miss the end of this game.

I turned just in time to see Darren snatch the ball from Deacon Harris, who looked genuinely confused. Graye ran after Darren, but he was too late. My baby ran down the court, and in the last twenty seconds, he shot a three-pointer that went in. Everyone shouted. The tie was broken, and the youth boys had won. Simone and I were up on our feet in an instant, running down to the court. I grabbed Darren and engulfed him in a bear hug. I knew I was acting like one of those mothers teenagers complain about, but I couldn't help it. I was just so proud of him. "Okay, Ma. I can't breathe." Darren squirmed, trying to get out of my embrace.

"Yeah, Leah, stop embarrassing my godson."

"Oh, Darren, don't let your godmother fool you. She was just as bad as I was while you were playing." Darren grinned at both of us as Malaysia came running over to us.

"Mommy, did you see me?"

"Yes, I saw you, baby, and I have to say you were the best little cheerleader out there." Darren tousled Malaysia's hair.

"Yeah, you were on point, Shorty." Malaysia smiled up at her big brother.

"And so were you."

"Hey, Darren." We all turned to see the rest of Darren's team waiting for him.

"Okay, Ma, it's pizza time."

"Yeah, me too, Mommy."

"You two go ahead, and don't eat too much pizza."

"Okay," they both said in unison as they both left to catch up with their friends.

About twenty minutes later, Simone, Adrian, and I were seated in the center's dining room, where all the adults were eating. Rain had to leave and assist with the children, who were in a different area of the center where they could eat and then play inside games. Everything had been set up nicely. Simone and I had helped with some of the decorations, and we'd tried to make it look festive. Each table had a different theme, and that table had decorations according to the theme. It looked very colorful and cheerful in here. "You ladies did a good job," Adrian complimented. The food looked great as well. While the kids had their choice of either pizza or hamburgers, we had the works. The long list of choices included ribs, fried chicken, grilled hot dogs, grilled steak, potato salad, macaroni and cheese, salad, corn on the cob, and a multitude of cakes and pies. "Now this is good eating." Simone and I laughed as Adrian dug into one of his two plates.

"Do you mind if I join you?" Why did that voice have such an effect on me?

"Sure, Graye, we don't mind." I shot Simone a seething look, and this time I hoped it worked. But with one look at her face, I could tell she was enjoying herself immensely.

Simone made the introductions between Graye and Adrian. They shook hands, and then Adrian stopped for moment as if in thought. "Graye Barrington? *The* Graye Barrington of Taylor Industries?"

"That would be me." Graye smiled.

"Hey man, you've got a really good company. I've had family and friends that have used your company to build. Not to mention all the people you employ." It was clear to see that Graye had instantly earned Adrian's respect. Suddenly, Simone's smile disappeared, and I turned to see what she was frowning at. Then I saw her. It was the woman who'd made the comment outside, and she was headed our way. Graye saw her coming and groaned. I almost laughed at his expression.

"Hi, Graye. I was trying to get your attention while you were heading over here, but I guess you didn't hear me. I saved you a seat over there." She pointed to some remote area in the corner. Graye turned toward the young lady and attempted to smile, but it didn't quite come off.

"Thank you, Sylvia, but I'm fine right here." Sylvia's smile disappeared. She shot me an evil look and then flounced away with an attitude. We all looked at each other for a moment, and when we couldn't hold it in any longer, we all burst out laughing.

For a while we enjoyed ourselves eating, laughing, and talking. And then I noticed a couple of uncomfortable stares from some of the members. Simone noticed as well, and as if on cue, everyone became quiet. Everyone accept Sylvia. I could hear her clear across the room. "No, I will not be quiet. She isn't even divorced yet, and look how she's throwing herself at Deacon Barrington. Somebody needs to stand up and say something. Look at her sitting over there with him like she's single." And if there had been anyone who wasn't already looking, now all eyes were on me. Instantly, I lost my appetite. Simone saw me move, and she grabbed my arm as if to keep me in place. Normally, I was a calm and rational person, but over the last few months, my emotions had been all over the place. Graye looked at me, and I could see the concern in his eyes.

"Leah, there is only one way to handle this, and in the long run, I pray you you'll understand. As I told you before, I am done hiding what I'm feeling. I'm going to stop this right now. And I'm going to stop it with the truth." *What truth is he talking about?* I opened my mouth to speak, but there were no words as Graye stood up and began to speak.

"Before I really get into this, let me say this." He turned to Sylvia for a moment. "Sylvia, you really need to work on that jealousy issue, and in the meantime I'll be praying for you on that." Now turning his back to her, he addressed the crowd. "Now, before all kinds of nasty rumors get started, let me set the record straight. Yes, it is true that I am falling in love with Leah Gordon." I could hear surprised gasps as Graye talked. "And yes, she is in the middle of a divorce, as Sylvia was so kind to point out. No, we are not having some type of sordid affair. Some of you will still believe what you will, but I will not stand by while lies are spread around about this amazing godly woman. She hasn't done anything to deserve this. And just to let you know, Leah has made it quite clear that all she can offer me is friendship. Being a true man of God, I am accepting that friendship despite what I really feel inside. So that's it, that's the truth.

"And this is true as well." Graye moved until he was facing only me. As he began to talk again, it was as if it were only he and I there instead of a room full of people. "Leah, I am falling in love with you. I even love time, as it takes on new meaning because of you. Days can pass by without me seeing you, and still the memory of the last time I saw you stays with me, comforts me. I am at peace because I know one day you will be *my* wife. I will wait patiently for months, years if I have to, because after the love of Jesus Christ, nothing compares to this love I have for you."

As Graye and I gazed at each other, two words replayed themselves over and over in my mind: *my wife.* Still in shock, I realized that at some point I had stood up. For a brief moment, it had seemed like it was just Graye and me here in our own little world. But now I became aware of my surroundings, and the harsh reality set in as I realized Graye had just confessed his love for me in front of the entire church. No one moved or made a single sound. Not knowing what else to do, I walked as quickly as I could to the door. I had to get out of here. As I walked out to leave, Pastor Richards was coming in. There wasn't even any point in being glad he hadn't witnessed this little drama, because I knew he would be told. "Hello, Leah. How are you?" I could only offer him a hint of a smile as I walked away.

"Leah, wait!" Simone ran to catch up with me. I didn't slow down. I kept walking, trying to put as much distance as I could between myself and the center. As I walked across the field to the parking lot, Simone fell in step beside me. We walked in silence. Once I reached my car, I stopped. I'd planned on just hopping in my car and leaving, but I couldn't leave without seeing Darren and Malaysia. They were officially with Granny for the summer now. I would be okay, I told myself. I would stand here and wait for the kids. "Um, Leah, this may not be the right time, but Graye wants to talk to you."

"Talk? Don't you think he just did enough of that? Why, Simone? Why did he do it? Did he tell you that?"

"Leah, it really isn't that bad. And what he did, he did to try and protect you. I mean, think about it. It's not all the time a woman can get a man to confess his undying love in front of a crowd of people. That really took some guts. I actually thought it was romantical."

"Romantical? Simone, that's not even a real word."

"Moving, then."

"Moving?"

"Yes, Leah, moving. Look, we've been friends too long to pretend. I know he affected you with the things he said, reason being, you feel the same way. Be honest; this is me now." This was my best friend, and I couldn't lie to her.

"Okay, okay. You're right. I do feel what he feels. But I'm not ready for this right now. Especially the part about being his wife." I looked at my friend for under-standing. "Simone, these feelings we have for each other, it scares me. It feels like nothing I've ever known with a man." She hugged me, and I hugged her back, thankful for the support.

"It's okay to admit you're scared sometimes. I even understand you not being ready for a relationship right now. You're still going through a divorce, and you have the right to take all the time you need. I just want you to be honest with yourself about how you feel about Graye. Once you do that everything, else will eventu-ally fall into place."

My wife. I just couldn't stop hearing those words in my ears. Everything he'd said had touched my heart. It was just so much to process all at once. "Simone, did he really say all those beautiful things to me?" I didn't have to look at her to know she was smiling.

"Yes, Leah, he said those things, and I'd bet any-thing he truly meant every word."

chapter 14

One year later, I was sitting on Granny's porch watching the kids play. I smiled as it made me think of when I was a child running around in this same yard. Life had been so simple then. These last several months, I'd thought of Graye often. I had seen him often in church and even when Taylor had her sessions, but I'd always kept our interactions friendly but short. It hadn't been easy, but I had had to put my feelings for him in the back of my mind as I'd dealt with court dates and mediations for the divorce. After that one night at the church, Bryce hadn't tried anything else, but he'd really screwed himself when he'd attacked me. The honorable Judge Daniel Brookstone frowned heavily upon domestic violence. And Veronica Sanchez was clearly dynamic outside the courtroom as well as in. She'd found other houses and other businesses that I hadn't had a clue about. Financially, my kids would never have to worry about anything. I couldn't believe I'd been so blind. I'd refused to see what was right before my eyes. But now my eyes were open, and I could see everything.

Glancing down at my lap, I looked at my divorce papers for a moment. It was finally over, and I felt an overwhelming sense of peace. I remembered that last day of court. I'd walked outside into the brilliant sunlight, and a sense of serenity had filled me even then. Walking down the steps of the courthouse, I'd smiled to myself because I knew it was nobody but Jesus who'd seen me through this entire situation. Looking toward the sky, I hadn't even realized that Bryce had fallen in step beside me. I'd looked at him with no anger—no fear, no hard feelings at all. Bryce, on the other hand, had looked deeply troubled, shocked even. "Bryce, are you okay?" I asked, truly concerned by the way he was looking.

"Leah, is this really happening? Are we really over?" His voice sounded shaky and unsure.

"Bryce we will always be connected because of Malaysia. But yes, you and I, *we* are over." And with that I'd walked away, leaving him behind.

"Didn't you say you had some errands to run today?" Granny stood inside the screen door, interrupting my thoughts. For some reason, I had the distinct impression she was trying to get rid of me. Normally she would have made her famous lemonade and we would have sat down and talked for hours about any and everything. But today was different. If I didn't know any better, I'd say she was acting nervous. "Are you trying to get rid of me?"

"Don't be silly, Leah, I just remember you having some things to do today, and I didn't want you to be late." I looked at her then. She really was acting strange. And that's when I saw it. I'd recognize that Hummer anywhere. It was Graye coming down the street. I watched as he pulled into Granny's driveway. "Close your mouth, girl, before a fly gets in there," Granny said, coming outside to sit in the chair across from me. I couldn't believe she was making a joke about this. I watched as Darren and Malaysia ran up to Graye's car. Taylor jumped out of the car and came running over to me. She hugged me tightly. And I was really happy to see her even though I didn't know why they were here. Hugging her back, I looked at Graye with questions in my eyes. Taylor, eager to get over to Darren and Malaysia, spoke to Granny briefly before running off. The three of us stood there in an awkward silence.

"Hello, Leah." Graye was the first to speak.

"Hello, Graye. How are you?" I had tried not to look into his eyes, but it was a battle that was soon lost. And once again, I found myself drowning.

"I'm fine, and yourself?"

"I'm fine." Minutes passed without anyone saying anything, and then finally Graye broke the silence.

"Well, Clara-Ann, I have that appointment in a little while, but I won't be long. Leah, it was good seeing you." He smiled at me before turning around and walking back to his car. He waved to the kids. All three waved back and then went back their conversation. This was the norm for them. What was I missing here? I looked at Granny suspiciously. I became even more suspicious as she suddenly stood up and headed back inside the house. "I'm going to make lemonade," she announced in a voice that left no room for argument. What was going on here? Oh, my little errands were just going to have to wait. I wasn't leaving until I got some straight answers.

Ten minutes later, Granny and I were sitting across from each other with glasses of lemonade. She'd even brought out the chocolate chip cookies. I had to smile at her attempt to soften me up. She knew I loved anything chocolate. "Okay, what's the deal? "What deal? I don't know what you're talking about." She was trying not to smile herself as she looked away from me.

"Oh, you know what I'm talking about. I can see it in your face." Sighing dramatically, she turned back toward me.

"Okay, you want to know; here it is. Graye and Taylor have been coming by for months. It started with a school assignment of Taylor's. It was her cooking class, and it was her turn to bring in a dish. Graye called me, and of course, I told him I would help. He brought her over, and Taylor and I had a good time. You know, she is a very sweet young lady. Anyway, the next day she took enough lasagna, salad, and garlic bread for the entire class, and they absolutely loved it. Since then, she's been coming over every weekend, and I teach her to cook something new. We have a routine. She and Graye come over, and she plays with the kids for a while. After a while, the girls come inside, and we cook while the boys play basketball down the street. And then we all eat together. So that's it, that's what's been going on."

Not quite knowing what to make of this, I stood up from the swing and walked over to the steps. All this had been going on, and I hadn't had any idea. No one had said anything. Standing there, I struggled with conflicting emotions. On one hand, I felt betrayed.

This was my family, and without my knowledge, Graye had integrated himself right in the mix. And why hadn't anyone said anything? It felt like some kind of conspiracy. On the other hand, I was happy to know that Taylor was opening up and expanding her world. Letting people in was a big step for her. And the fact that Graye had been spending time with Darren really touched me. A bond had been formed between my family and his almost as naturally as if it had been destined all along. Lastly, I felt left out. Where did this all leave me?

"Leah, I have to admit, I've been encouraging Graye to come around with Taylor."

"Why?"

"Because I can see things you can't. Leah, this man is a man of God who loves you to no end. He's waiting patiently for you to give him some kind of sign, some kind of hope that there is a future for the two of you."

"Have you forgotten that I've just divorced my husband of ten years?"

"Yes, but that was the man that *you* chose. Graye is the man that God chose for you. And even though he and Taylor have been here with me and the kids having a good time, there has been something missing."

"And what might that something be?"

"You," she said as she took the empty lemonade glasses inside the house.

With everything that had been going on, I'd basically cut off all communication between Graye and myself. When I did see him in church, I was always polite yet distant. After the picnic, I'd really needed some time to figure things out. Graye had respected that and had given me the distance I'd needed. I hadn't told anyone, but I'd realized that day at the picnic I was in love with Graye. I just wasn't sure how to handle it. And then there was the divorce. I had needed that entire situation to be over and done with. Now that it was done, there was really nothing standing in the way. And today when I'd seen Graye, it made me realize how much I'd missed him. I'd actually wanted to run into his arms and never leave. Could we be a family? I didn't know, but I did know that I'd like to try. I wasn't sure what was going to happen, but figuring things out with Graye seemed a lot more appealing than this self-induced torture I'd been putting myself through being without him. There hadn't been a day that he hadn't been in my thoughts. And now Granny was telling me he still felt the same way about me. The sheer happiness of that threatened to overtake me.

Over the next few weeks, I conveniently showed up at Granny's when Graye and Taylor were there. I didn't interrupt her cooking lessons. I felt that the cooking and life lessons were things that Taylor could use to blossom even more. I could see the bond the two of them had formed, and it warmed my heart to see Taylor growing and opening up this way. It was also great to see Laysia with them. She was the eager assistant, and it didn't matter if she was cracking eggs or gathering ingredients; she took her job very seriously. Sitting outside with my lemonade, I had a clear view of Graye with the boys as they played basketball. They really looked up to him, especially Darren, and surprisingly, that didn't scare me anymore. He really cared, and he was having such a positive influence with my children and also with the youth in the church. As time went on, I became more and more impressed with this true man of God.

The next couple of months flew by as Graye and I spent more and more time together. The kids had now started school again, but we still managed to spend a lot of time over at Granny's. Taylor had become another welcome extension at Granny's house. Gone was the scared little girl afraid to let anyone in. Before my eyes, Taylor grew confident and unafraid of life. We'd grown even closer. And Graye, he was amazing, unlike any man I had ever known before. We never spoke the actual words but with one look you could tell how we felt about each other. Sometimes I felt torn. I knew I was divorced now, but I was still counseling Taylor. I didn't want to do anything that would cause her to have a setback. While I could tell she loved all of us being together, I didn't know what the outcome was going to be between Graye and I, and I didn't want her to get hurt. I was falling for him, and I was going to have to figure out what I was going to do about it.

One night while we were having dinner, I ran into the kitchen to get more drinks, and when I came back to the doorway, I stopped for a moment and watched as Graye joked around with all three kids. They laughed at his antics. I could've turned the movie off, and no one would have even noticed. In that moment, I realized I was in love with this man and this wasn't just going to fade away.

As I walked into the room, Graye's cell phone rang. He wasn't even paying attention. Grabbing the phone off the table, I walked over and handed it to a smiling Graye. . "Hello? Wait; calm down, Carl. *What?*" My heart pounding, I took Graye by the hand and led him out of the room. Granny, who had been sitting on the porch, came in when she heard Graye's voice. "Carl, did anyone get hurt? Okay, good. I'll be there in five minutes." Graye hung up the phone and looked at me frantically. "Baby, I've got to go."

"Graye, you're scaring me. What happened?"

"Some maniac has just set one of my warehouses on fire. Thank God no one was there tonight." Grabbing his keys, he kissed me on the forehead. I promise I'll call you when I get there."

"Graye, I'm going with you," I told him, putting on my shoes. "Granny, will you watch the kids, please?"

"Leah, you know you don't have to ask that. Those children will be just fine here." I stood up after putting on my shoes. Graye stood in the doorway, blocking my path.

"Leah, I don't want you anywhere near a fire. Now, just stay here, and I'll call you when I get there."

"Graye, you can park as far away as you'd like to keep me from the fire, but I'm going with you." He wanted to argue, but both of us were aware that he was wasting time.

"Okay, let's go," he said with a sigh.

Five minutes later, we were there. Graye parked in a vacant parking lot across the street from the warehouse. Getting out of the car, we both stood there in shock and disbelief as we watched the flames. The fire department hadn't gotten here yet. Carl came running over to us. "Hey, man, thanks for calling me. You did say no one was in there, right?" And that's when I saw it.

At the corner of the building was Bryce's car. "From what I can tell, no one is. But I'm not sure who's car that is over there," he said, pointing to Bryce's car. "I know. I know whose car that is," I said to Graye as my cell phone began to ring. I continued to look at him as I answered.

"Hello?" The voice on the other end was barely more than a whisper, and I had to strain to hear.

"Leah, it's me. You've got to help me. Look, I'm sorry, but I don't want to die in here. Please help me—"

"Bryce, Bryce!" I yelled into the phone, but he was gone.

"Leah, is that Bryce? What did he say? Did he do this?" How could I tell him? How could Bryce still be in there? *This can't be happening.* Turning to Graye, I looked up at him with tears in my eyes.

"It's Bryce, Graye, and that was him on the phone. He's still in there. He must have set the fire and then gotten trapped somehow."

"Bryce?" Graye asked as if he couldn't believe it himself.

"Man, I had no idea anyone was in there. I called the police and the fire department. They'll be here any minute," Carl said.

"He won't make it that long." Graye looked at the fire as flames engulfed the building. Turning back to me, Graye took me in his arms and hugged me. Instantly I felt guilty. This was my fault. And here he was still trying to protect me. As if reading my mind, Graye stepped back for a moment and tilted my face with his finger until I was looking into his eyes. "Leah, this is not your fault. Do you hear me? You are not the blame for this. I love you, and right now I need you to make me a promise." I didn't like the sound of this at all as I looked into his determined eyes.

"Promise me, Leah, that if anything happens to me, you'll take Taylor."

"Of course I will. But what are you talking about?"

Grabbing my face and kissing me, he stepped back. "I have to go in there Leah."

"No," I screamed, grabbing his shirt.

"Baby, I have to. He could die by the time help gets here."

"No," I screamed again. I was hysterical now and refused to let go of him. He looked at Carl for help. Carl stepped in and gently yet firmly took me by the arms. Carl looked at Graye doubtfully.

"Man, are you sure you want to do this? Help should be here any minute. Besides, isn't he the one that set the place on fire?" It was clear to see that Carl didn't agree with Graye's decision either.

"I know what he did, but he's in there. And if I just stand by and do nothing, what kind of man of God does that make me?" Looking at me one last time, he smiled bravely. "I love you, Leah." And then he was gone into the smoke, into the fire.

Crying uncontrollably now, I sank to the ground and helplessly leaned against the car. Carl, unsure of what to say, just stood there as we both watched the fire destroy the building. In the distance, I could hear the sirens. Looking toward the sky, I prayed. *Please, God. Please bring both of them out of this alive. Please bring Graye back to me.* I could feel the heat, even though I was across the street. And then I watched in horror as the windows at the top of the building burst, sending glass everywhere. Standing up now, I began to pace. "There! There he is," Carl shouted, pointing to a shadowy figure. Through the smoke, I could barely make him out as Graye walked toward us. I didn't see anyone walking with him. As he neared us, I could see him clearly now. And the sight of Graye as he carried an unconscious Bryce took my breath away. My heart flowed with an overpowering love for this man who had just risked his life. Carl ran to help Graye the rest of the way. They gently laid Bryce down as we waited for the ambulance to come. Seconds later, the police, fire department, and the ambulance arrived.

Hours later, I was still fussing over Graye. We were at my house. After calling Granny to check on the kids, who were all sleeping, we'd decided to stay here. Graye took my hand in a calming gesture. "Baby, they already checked me out at the hospital. I am fine." I knew he was, but I couldn't help myself. I began to shake, and Graye pulled me close to him and held me. I couldn't stop the shaking, and he seemed to understand. I still couldn't believe it. I couldn't believe Bryce had set the fire. I couldn't believe Graye had gone in that same fire and saved Bryce. It was just all too much. Graye held me for a long time, and at some point, I realized he'd fallen asleep. Maneuvering myself out of his grasp, I eased him down onto the couch until his head rested on a pillow. Going to the hall closet, I got a blanket and laid it over him. When the phone rang, I grabbed it quickly and went into the kitchen so as not to disturb Graye.

"Leah, are you okay? I just saw the news. How is Graye?" It was Simone.

"I am fine. I think we're both going to be okay," I said, sitting down at the kitchen table. "Simone, I just can't help feeling this is my fault. I never in a million years thought Bryce would do something like this. And then Graye going in to save him like that. I could've lost him. I can't help thinking I could have prevented this somehow."

"And how could you have done that? You had no way of knowing Bryce was going to snap and go psycho."

"You know, that last day of court I saw him outside, and he didn't look right."

"Yeah, but no one would have thought he'd do what he did tonight. You can't take that blame on yourself. And what does Graye say?"

"He just says he loves me and it's not my fault. I love him, Simone, but I don't want him hurt."

"Well, if it's Bryce you're worried about, you can let that go. From the way it sounds on the news, after he get's out of the hospital, he's either going to jail or a psych ward somewhere. Believe me, you and Graye are the least of his worries right now."

"Leah, do you remember the special dinner at Clara-Ann's last year? It was the day you finally told your mother and Clara-Ann what was going on with you and Bryce."

"Yes, I remember," I said. My smile was bittersweet at the memory of that day.

"You said you laughed, talked, ate, and just had a good time being with family. It felt like home."

"Yes?"

"Well, let me ask you a question. Was Graye there that day?" And then it struck me what she was trying to say. Even then, Graye had been there, bringing me happiness and making me smile. He'd fit right in, as if he were a part of my life, a part of my family. He was home.

A week later, I was home. The kids were with Granny. I had checked on Graye, and he was resting at home. I smiled in anticipation of having the day completely to myself. I sat down on the couch with a glass of lemonade and a book to read. A moment later the doorbell rang. I opened the door and was pleasantly surprised to see that it was Taylor.

"Hi, how did you get here?" I peered over her shoulder to see a woman and another teenager sitting in a silver Honda accord in my driveway. The woman waved at me and I waved back and smiled. "Who is that, Taylor?"

She walked in and closed the door. "That's my friend Kenya and her mother, Sonya. We are going to the movies, but we are a little early, so I asked if I could stop here first." She smiled shyly as she looked at me. She had something to say, and I would let her say it when she was ready. My heart soared with just the fact that she was making friends now and trusting people. "I have really come to love our sessions, and I have learned so much from you over this last year. I feel, though, that I don't need the counseling anymore. I feel better than I have in a long time, and I'm just ready to move on. I still want to be friends."

I was so proud of this young lady standing before me. She was so strong and happy now. "Of course we will be friends but I want you to be sure. Have you discussed this with Graye?"

"Yes, and he says the decision is mine to make and he will support me."

"Well, okay then. I feel you have opened up and dealt with everything remarkably. I will always be here if you need me. You know that." She smiled again and hugged me.

"I know." A minute later I walked her out, and when she got to the car, she looked back at me. "Nothing can stop you and Uncle Graye now," she said, and with that, she got in the car. Stunned, I stood there for a moment as they drove away. I had tried my best to be discreet, but Taylor had been too smart for us and she hadn't missed a thing.

I smiled to myself and closed the door just as the phone began to ring.

"Hello?"

"Leah, it's me, Graye." Closing my eyes, I smiled. Even the sound of him saying my name made me happy.

"Yes?"

"Do you know where the new bookstore is downtown?"

What a strange question. "Well, yes, I mean I haven't been there. But I know where it is. Why?"

"Can you meet me there in twenty minutes?" Suddenly filled with anticipation, I did my best to make my voice sound normal.

"Yes, I can meet you, but are you going to tell me what this is all about?"

"I'll see you in twenty minutes, okay?" He didn't give me a chance to ask any more questions as he hung up.

This day was turning out to be full of surprises and suddenly I didn't want to spend it alone. I had no idea what this was all about; I just knew I wanted to be with Graye. If he wanted to bookshop today, then we would book shop together.

Once downtown, I quickly parked. As I began walking to the bookstore, I told myself to calm down. I felt like I was sixteen again on my very first date. In the distance, I could see Graye standing in front of the bookstore. Immediately I felt butterflies in my stomach. *Girl, get some kind of control,* I told myself. I walked over to the bookstore, and we stood there for a moment looking at each other. I wondered if it would always be like this, this speaking to each other without words.

Graye took my hand, I thought to lead me into the bookstore. "Do you trust me, Leah?"

"Yes, Graye, I do." And I did. Despite everything I'd gone through, I really did trust Graye. It was everything about him, but most importantly, it was the way I could see Christ in him.

"Close your eyes for a moment, Leah." Honoring his request, I closed my eyes and let him lead me away. After a moment, we stopped. Still I kept my eyes closed, even though the suspense was killing me. I could hear keys. *Keys?* And then we were moving forward again. "Step up, Leah." As soon as I stepped up, he pulled me forward. As I moved forward, the sweet smell of chocolate hit me. "Okay, open your eyes." I opened my eyes and was shocked to see that we weren't in a bookstore at all. I was standing right in the middle of the most delicious-looking chocolate shop I'd ever seen. There was chocolate of every single kind here. But it wasn't the chocolate that made tears spring to my eyes. The entire shop was lit with candles. Walking further into the room, I noticed the roses. They were everywhere—on the counters, the floor. Not believing what I was seeing, I turned around in the middle of the room, taking everything in. With tears in my eyes, I turned to Graye. I could tell from the expression on his face, he was loving my reaction.

"What did you do?" I asked him tearfully. Before answering, he took my hand again and led me even further into the room. To the left of us, in the corner, was a beautiful little table meant for two. The table was already set. There was a candle lit on each side, and in the middle of the table were two long-stemmed roses in a small vase. There was also a covered dish on each side. I didn't know what was under those tops, but at the moment, I was too thrilled to eat anything. Walking around, Graye pulled out my chair so I could sit down.

We just sat there looking at each other for a moment. "You asked me what I did. Well, Leah, I fell in love. Months ago, a beautiful woman captured my heart, and she hasn't let it go ever since." The intensity of Graye's eyes only deepened as he continued. "I watched this amazing woman face heartache and pain, and my love for her only grew. And then I met her children, and I love them." Hearing him say he loved my children did something incredible inside me. I felt as if I were going to burst with happiness from the inside out. "As I said before, I am rebuilding what another man tried to tear down. I love you, Leah. That's what I did; that's what I'm always going to do." Smiling, he reached for my hand across the table, and we sat there holding hands. I wasn't ready to talk yet, and he seemed to accept this. "So if you had to name the place, what would you name it?"

Staring at him for a moment, I could feel the butterflies again as I began to comprehend what he was getting at.

"What do you mean if I had to name the place? Graye, you rented this place for the night, right?" I could hear the nervousness in my voice as I spoke.

"Not quite."

"Graye are you saying you bought this shop?"

"Yes. I bought it, Leah, but not for me. This is your shop."

What? I stared at him in disbelief. "Graye, you didn't."

"Yes, I did. It's yours to do with as you wish."

"But why? I don't even know what to say."

"In our marriage and life together, there will be many different ways in which I will show my love for you. This is just one of those ways. You love chocolate, and I love you." Months ago, I'd thought it would be years before I'd be in another relationship. And marriage? I hadn't thought that was a possibility at all. But looking at this man sitting across from me, I was believing in things I hadn't believed in, in a long time. "Okay, let's eat." Graye removed the tops of the covered dishes. I laughed when I saw the single piece of chocolate in the middle of the huge dish.

Picking up the chocolate, I took a bite. I closed my eyes as the mixture of chocolate and caramel filled my mouth. My eyes still closed, I chewed slowly, savoring the delicious taste. Moments later, I opened my eyes to find Graye staring at me. The smile I'd seen on his face just minutes ago was now gone. He looked totally serious now. "Graye, what's wrong?"

"Leah, it is true that I am a man of God, but I am also human. So whatever you do, don't ever eat chocolate in front of me again until we are married."

"Why?"

"Because I am so tempted to kiss you." The urgent need to kiss him took over, and I leaned across the table. What I meant to be a light kiss turned into an explosion of emotion. The moment our lips touched, the world as I'd known it ceased to exist as I was spun into a world of pure magic. Time stopped as we kissed, and I realized I never wanted this kiss or this night to end. Slowly and passionately, our tongues began their dance. I had started this kiss, but now it was Graye who took over and swept me away into another world. I felt myself open up as I tried to express everything in this kiss I hadn't been able to say in actual words. "I hear you, and I love you too," he said finally, ending the kiss.

"I don't want to, but we've got to stop. I want us to do this right, and if we keep kissing, something is going to happen tonight." I knew he was right, and I was glad one of us had been able to stop. Kissing me on the forehead, he excused himself for a moment and went outside. Walking back over to the middle of the room, I sat down in a bed of rose petals. Stretching out my arms, I let the soft red petals move through my hands. Looking around the room again, I could see he'd put a lot of thought and care into this; the setting was mystical. When Graye walked back into the shop, I reached out my hand for him to come sit with me. He sat behind me and pulled me against him, making me feel warm and safe. "All three children are sleeping, so there's no worries there. And Granny told me to make sure you get home safely. So whenever you're ready, just let me know."

"Let's just sit here for a few more minutes. Then we can leave, okay?"

"Okay." I let myself relax in his embrace, and we sat there like that for a while. I loved the feel of him holding me. Once again, I closed my eyes. So this is what it felt like to truly be cared for by a man. For the second time, I wished the night would never end.

An hour later, we were standing in front of my house, saying good night. I knew he had to leave, but as we stood there hugging, I found it almost impossible to separate myself from his warm embrace. In his embrace, I found love and strength. Something inside said it was okay to love this man freely, holding nothing back. He kissed me again and started toward his car. "I'll see you tomorrow."

"Okay. Graye?"

"Yes, Leah?" he said, turning to face me and smiling that smile that always seemed to make me melt.

"I love you." I watched the emotions working in his face. I was happy to know that my words affected him in the same way his had affected me. He'd always been the one to tell me how he felt about me. This was the first time I'd said those three little words to him, and I could clearly see me telling him how I truly felt was what he'd been waiting for.

"I love you too, Leah." I watched as he drove away. Sighing, I went into the house.

My only real concern now was the children. How would they take me dating another man? Even though they knew Bryce and I were divorced, I didn't know if they were ready for this. After that night at the chocolate shop, I'd asked Graye to give me a few days to talk to the kids and let them know about us before we officially went public with our relationship. He thought we should talk to them together, but I wanted to talk to them first. He was very understanding and patient. That was one more thing I would have to get used to. It was like I'd actually written a letter to God, listing all the things I needed in a man, and He'd sent me Graye. And every time I prayed to God about Graye and I, I would feel a sense of peace and this amazing love that seemed to radiate straight from God right down to Graye and me.

Now that I knew how I truly felt about Graye, I just hoped the children would accept it, and I hoped that they would come to love him as well. I didn't have long to wait because about a week later, I found out exactly how my children felt about Graye and I. We'd just finished eating dinner at Granny's, and the kids had gone out to the living room while Granny and I cleaned the kitchen. While we were finishing the kitchen, both Darren and Malaysia came into the kitchen and stood there. Granny and I glanced at each other and stopped what we were doing. They looked serious. "What's up, you two?" I asked with an eyebrow raised.

"Mama, Laysia and I would like to have a family meeting."

"Okay, and what about, might I ask?"

"Can we all go to the living room, please?" I almost laughed at my son's seriousness, but I didn't want to hurt his feelings. I could tell this was important to him. Turning, I smiled at Granny.

"Are you joining us for the family meeting?"

"I wouldn't miss this for the world," she said, following us out of the kitchen.

We all chose a couch and sat down. I sat and waited for Darren to start. "Ma, we want to know how you feel about Graye." Granny laughed and shook her head as I gave her a look pleading for help. Taking a deep breath, I faced my children.

"I'll be honest with you both, I really like Graye. He's a good and kind man. But I'm really interested in knowing how the two of you feel about him." They looked at each other for a moment before Darren spoke again.

"We like him. He's the real deal, I can tell. And it would just be kind of nice, you know."

"What would be kind of nice?"

"It would just be nice to have a real-deal man around. Plus, he makes you smile, Ma." I really looked at my son then. He looked back at me with an awareness that seemed beyond his age. Children were so perceptive these days.

"Well, Malaysia, you've been quiet. Do you have anything to add to this?"

"Well, if you're not going to be with Daddy, then Graye—I mean, Mr. Barrington, is the next best choice. I like him, Mommy. And I like Taylor too."

"Okay, well, thank you for calling this family meeting. You both really helped Mommy make a decision."

Feeling as if a weight had been lifted, I hugged them both.

"Now that that's settled, who wants dessert?" Granny asked as she got up to go into the kitchen.

"I do," we all chimed in and followed her into the kitchen.

Later that night, I went home on a natural high. Humming to myself, I unlocked the front door and went inside the house. Hearing the phone ringing, I quickly locked the door and ran to the living room to get the phone. "Hello?"

"Hello, Leah, it's me." It was simply amazing how his voice could instantly make me smile. It had only been a couple of days since I'd talked to him, but it had seemed like forever.

"Graye, how are you?"

"Well, I've missed you, but other than that I'm good. And you?"

"Well, I've missed you too, but I'm much better now that I've talked to the kids. No, let me rephrase that. *They* talked to *me*."

"And what did they say?" he asked, intrigued. Smiling to myself, I curled up on the comfortable couch and began to tell him about my conversation with the kids. "So they like me. Well, we're all in luck because I already love them. And with time, I hope they grow to love me as well."

"I know they will, Graye. I love you." It was so easy for me to say it now. It was time for me to stop struggling with my feelings for him. It was okay to love again. To love this deeply could only come from God.

chapter 15

"So what about you? Have you talked to Taylor about us?" I was anxious to know what she thought of us being together. "Yes, I did, and she is on cloud nine. She can't wait for us all to start doing things together. Leah, I know we'll never take the place of the mother she lost, but I think with our families combined, we can offer Taylor a chance at a real family life again." A wave of complete euphoria came over me. Graye always warmed my heart with the things he said and did. And I knew deep down inside, he meant every word he said. The things he did were honest and true illustrations of his love for me.

"I feel the same way," I told him.

An hour later, I was still floating from my conversation with Graye when I reached for the phone again to call Simone. She'd left a week ago to attend a wedding in New York. I had missed my friend, and I couldn't wait to tell her everything that had happened. As I reached for the phone, it rang. "Hello?"

"Girl, it's me. Are you sitting down? I have something to tell you."

"You must have read my mind, because I was just about to call you."

"Okay, sit down, because, girl, you are not going to believe what I am about to tell you."

"What? What's going on, Simone?"

"Are you sitting down?"

"Simone!"

"Okay, okay. Well, today Adrian and I were eating lunch at *Carabas* and—"

"Wait, you and Adrian? Again? If I didn't know any better I'd say you two were a couple again."

"We weren't a couple the first time, okay."

"Oh, so you admit it, now you are."

"Yes, I mean no. Wait; stop distracting me. We'll get back to that in a minute. Listen to me. Are you listening?"

"Yes, I'm listening."

"Okay, we were eating lunch and Adrian's cell phone rang. Guess who it was? Sean Gregory, his detective friend." She had my complete attention now. I had been standing, but now I sat down and prepared myself. With everything that I'd found out in the last four months, who knew what she was going to tell me now. "Sean had an interesting visit this afternoon. Guess who came to see him?"

"Who?"

"You're not going to believe it, because I could hardly believe it myself when Adrian told me and—"

"*Simone!*"

"It was Angela Walters."

"What? Why was she there?"

"She hired him. She thinks Bryce is cheating on her."

"What? Already? Stop playing with me."

"You know I wouldn't joke about something like this. It's true. Well, since Bryce was released on bail, he and Angela have been living it up at her place. Well, for the past two weeks, Bryce has been coming in from work later and later. She says when he is there and his cell goes off, he quickly leaves the room like he's hiding something." I began to laugh then. It was all so ludicrous. Angela Walters had hired a private detective because Bryce was cheating on her now. I couldn't stop laughing. Just thinking of her paying money to hire a detective to spy on a man who'd just gotten a divorce for cheating on his wife was absolutely hilarious.

"Leah, Leah! Are you all right?"

"This really is a lifetime movie." Simone joined me in laughing then. It was so crazy that laughing was all we could do. "I'm fine, Simone. In fact, I am more than fine. It's just complete confirmation that I made the right decision in divorcing Bryce. You know, one day we were all at Granny's, just eating, talking, laughing, and having a good time. It just felt like family, like home, and I realized that at my own home it hadn't been like that with Bryce, not for a long time. Even the kids had gotten used to him being gone. Initially, they were upset when he left, but they have adjusted so well. And you know why? It's because he disappeared years ago. Mentally, he just dropped out of our lives. The affair was just the icing on the cake. But that's all in the past now. I have moved on. I have my children."

God has also blessed me to have you, Granny, my mother and now Graye.

I heard a sound on the other end that sounded like a cough and a laugh at the same time, and I remembered I still had to tell her everything. She didn't even know about my new shop, which I'd decided to name Chocolates by Barrington. "What did you just say?" Now I had her full attention.

"Oh we have a lot to talk about. Are you coming over here? Or am I coming over there?"

"Girl, I'll be there in five minutes. Get the popcorn ready."

"Oh and, Simone?"

"Yes?"

"Don't think you're getting off the hook."

"What?"

"We are going to talk about Graye *and* Adrian."

Three weeks later, I raced around my bedroom trying to get ready. Simone would be here any minute. I was looking forward to this. Girls' night out. It was going to be me, Simone, Rain, and Brooke. We were going to see that same play that I was supposed to see on my anniversary with Bryce. That all seemed so long ago now, I thought as I put on my earrings. Things had changed; life had changed, and all for the better. I glanced at a picture of Graye and me on my nightstand. Recently, we'd gone to the fair and taken pictures while we were there. In the picture, we looked happy and in love. This weekend, Graye was out of town attending a business meeting at one of his companies. He'd only been gone a couple of days, and I missed him like crazy. Only two more days and he'd be home. Smiling, I ran to answer the phone as it rang. "Hey, Leah, are you almost ready?"

"I'm almost ready. Hey, do you think it's best if I just meet you there?"

"No," she yelled. "I mean no. I'll be there in a few minutes. Tonight you are getting the full star treatment, okay?"

"Okay," I said. Exactly five minutes later, my doorbell rang. I opened up the door, and Simone rushed inside. Looking me over, she whistled. I was wearing a sparkling black creation that really showed off my figure. "If Graye could see you now."

"Hey, you don't look so bad yourself." I admired her dress. The short gold showstopper was another original Vera Wang.

"I admit it, we're both looking pretty good tonight." I laughed as she spun around and pretended to walk the runway. "Are you ready," she asked after she was done putting on her show. I grabbed my purse and headed for the door. I opened the door and my mouth dropped open.

She hadn't been kidding about the star treatment. There sitting in my driveway was a beautiful, white Lincoln Navigator limousine. I turned around and looked at Simone in surprise. She laughed at the expression on my face. "Girl, what did you do?"

"I told you, tonight is your night."

"My night?" Simone looked nervous suddenly. "I mean *our* night. Girl, let's go before we're late." I locked the door and walked to the limo. I could hear laughter inside. Rain and Brooke were already having a good time. Yes, tonight was our night, and I was sure it was going to be a night to remember.

The play was just getting started as we arrived. Silently, we crept to our seats so as not to disturb anyone else. Once I was settled in my seat, it wasn't long before I was completely entranced with the play. It was about a woman who had lost her first love and found him again years later. For the next two hours, I laughed and cried. The entire cast was good, but it was the main character, Alyssa, who drew you in, making you feel her joy and her pain. Glancing at my friends, I could see they were just as into this as I was. Turning back to the play, I watched the end in anticipation on whether or not Alyssa was going to keep her love. My heart leaped for joy when Alyssa's love, Eric, got down on one knee and took her hand. But instead of speaking directly to Alyssa, he looked out into the audience. I leaned forward as he began to speak. "Leah, I love you." *Leah? Did he just say my name?* I looked at Simone, who was still watching the play. I must be imagining things, I thought as I turned back to the play.

"I am a better man because of you, and I can't imagine life without you. Leah, will you marry Graye?" Then Eric stood up, and the entire cast came to the center of the stage and bowed. Everyone began to clap and cheer. I sat frozen in my seat. I was scared to tell my friends that I was having hallucinations. There was no way he had just said what I thought he'd said. The cast bowed one last time and then looked out into the audience as if they were looking for someone. One by one, they held out a hand as they turned to me. "Leah, will you marry Graye?" they all asked. Okay, so I wasn't hallucinating. Looking at Simone, I demanded an explanation.

"Simone, what is going on here?"

She simply patted my hand the way you would an anxious child, "Leah, everything will be clear in just a moment. I looked at Brooke and Rain, but they only smiled as if they knew a secret and weren't going to tell. Sighing, I looked toward the stage again, only to see the cast was gone. I watched in astonishment as about thirty children dressed as angels filled the stage. They were a beautiful sight to see. Their white costumes held almost a mystical glow to them, making the children look like real live angels. They all lined up, their small faces smiling with excitement. Each child held a single rose. *Leah, will you marry Graye?* The words danced around in my head. And then it began to dawn on me.

He was really asking me to marry him. And he was doing it in a way that was beyond my wildest dreams. He'd always been full of surprises, and tonight was another spectacular example of that. When our song began to play, I closed my eyes in sheer bliss. Oh, I loved this man so. It was like a dream I never wanted to wake up from. The children began to exit the stage one by one. I felt tears in my eyes as each child walked over to hand me a rose and asked their question, "Will you marry Graye?" As they handed me a rose and asked their question, they left the room. By the time the children were done, I had over two dozen roses. But I didn't have to worry. Simone had come prepared. I watched in astonishment as she pulled out two lovely vases and handed them to Rain and Brooke, who busied themselves with the roses. After the last child had left, the lights came on. I stood up, looking for Graye.

chapter 16

Instead of seeing Graye, I began to recognize faces. My mother and Granny. And beside them were Darren, Taylor, and Malaysia. Everyone began to stand up, and I realized I knew just about everyone in here. The entire church was here, including Pastor Richards and his wife, Carol. I wiped tears from my eyes as more and more people became recognizable. They clapped and cheered in my shocked happiness. I really wanted to see Graye now. As if hearing my thoughts, the lights dimmed again and a single light shone on the stage. And then he walked into clear view. I wanted to run up on the stage and throw myself into his arms. Everyone became quiet as he began to speak. "Before you answer that question, Leah, I'd like to show you this." And then he was gone again. I watched as the biggest projection screen came down from the ceiling.

Granny came alive on the screen, and I watched in fascination as she talked. "Well, Leah, I have to say that is some young man you have there. When he first approached me with this elaborate marriage proposal, I looked at him as if he'd bumped his head." The crowd laughed, myself included. Granny had always had a way with words. "But as he talked about his big plans, one thing was clear to me. See, like his plans, his love for you is big! And that's simple enough. When I saw all that love, I had no choice but to approve and help him in any way I could. And let me tell you, it wasn't easy. This play you've wanted to see for about a year now, they were done for the year. Graye had to pay dearly to have them perform one last time, especially since he wanted to alter the ending slightly. Yes, girl, he is the one." Once again, everyone broke into laughter. I was laughing and crying at the same time.

"I can tell your life together is really going to be an adventure. While making his plans, he also found time to do this." Granny was gone, and now on the screen I saw land and what looked like the beginnings of a home being built. I felt a shiver of excitement climbing up my spine. The camera zoomed in, and I could see lots of people there, walking, talking, carrying materials, and working. The camera zoomed in even closer, and I could hear Graye's voice. "Hey, Darren, you guys come over here and talk to your mother." Darren, Malaysia, and Taylor stopped what they were doing and came running. Then I was looking into their faces as Graye asked them questions.

"So, Darren, what do you all think of this?"

"What? Oh, this is cool. I mean, I don't see myself doing all this mushy stuff for *my* girl, but this is cool for you and Ma." We all laughed then. He had no idea what he was in for the day he truly fell in love. "And this house, this is your dream house, Mama. Like I told you before, he's the real deal." I felt a rush of exhilaration as my suspicions were confirmed—Graye was building this house for us. When I'd fallen in love with Graye, I'd never have guessed in a million years that he'd try to make all my dreams come true. I'd always wanted to build a home from the ground up—he knew that—and now he was making it happen.

I could also see that he'd gotten everyone involved. I now recognized church members, friends, and family on the video. Next were Taylor and Malaysia in front of the camera. "Well, I love it that we're doing this. I mean, I get a little sister, I get a brother, and just a new family altogether." Taylor laughed as she hugged Malaysia. She then grew serious as she looked into the camera.

"Leah, we dropped the doctor, and now I just call you Leah. But I was hoping that maybe one day I could call you Mom. If that's okay with you. See the way I figure it is, I have two mothers. My real mother went to heaven, and she still watches over me as one of God's angels. But God loves me so much, he sent me another mom to watch over me while I'm still here." I felt Simone squeeze my hand as I felt tears on my face once again. I looked over at Taylor, and she was crying herself. Starting to get up to go over to her, Simone stopped me. "Wait, watch this, Leah." I watched as friends and family sent messages of love and well wishes for Graye and me. Someone even said they hoped we'd have more children. Simone and I raised an eyebrow on that last one. By the time the video ended, half the room was sniffling and in tears. I was in awe of this beautiful man in my life.

Once the screen went up, a single light shone on the stage, and Graye walked out onto the stage. "I want to say thank you to everyone who was a part of this and made it happen. I couldn't have done this without your love and support. Thank you, and now if you'll excuse me, I have to get an answer to an important question." He walked off the stage and began to walk toward me. Aware of only him, I moved past Simone to meet him in the aisle. I couldn't stop the tears as I walked toward him. There were no words that could truly describe what I was feeling as I walked toward the love of my life. This was the kind of thing that happened in movies, and yet it was real. It was happening to me. Seconds later, I was in his arms, and it really was like coming home. Never wanting to let go, I held on tight. I have no idea how long we stood like that as the whole world melted away.

Eventually I felt him pulling away, but only so he could get down on one knee. My heart beat a mile a minute as he pulled out a little black box. I laughed when I looked at it, because it wasn't the traditional ring box. It was a small chocolate candy box. But when he opened it, there was no candy inside. I heard intakes of breath all around me as Graye took out the most exquisite, absolutely flawless, princess diamond engagement ring I had ever seen. It was absolutely breathtaking. My hand shook as he placed it on my finger. It had to be at least three karats. Looking down, I could see it was a perfect fit, *just like the man*, I thought, looking into his eyes.

"Leah, I saw you for the first time in church, and somewhere after the offering and before the benediction, I fell in love. I saw your face, and you were having your own personal conversation with God. I knew something had hurt you, and I knew right then I wanted to be a part of the healing. So I prayed to God and asked him for direction. He told me to wait, be patient, and He would let me know when it was our time. God had something so deep in mind for you and me, and that is why on that same first day I felt something inside that was so incredible and spiritual at the same time. It was like the meeting of souls. God wanted you to have a man who can and will pray your troubles away. A man anointed by Him and chosen for you to create a spiritual bond that is unbreakable." Graye, visibly emotional now, took my hand and kissed me gently on the lips as he looked into my eyes. And like so many times before, I found myself drowning again. "And in you, He chose a beautiful woman who takes my breath away every time I look at her. You are my gift in so many ways, and I thank God for sending me a woman who is strong, a woman who will pray *for* me and *with* me. At the same time, you possess a beauty and a grace that I am almost in awe of. Leah, this is us, this is our foundation. I did big things today, but simply, I love you, and I just want to spend the rest of my life with you. Will you marry me?"

"Yes, Graye, I love you, and I'll marry you," I said, flinging my arms around his neck and kissing him. The sound of cheers from the crowd was almost deafening. I could tell that we'd made everyone here truly happy with the news. But no one was happier than me. I hugged and kissed my husband to be. Smiling back at him, I knew without a single doubt that I would spend the rest of my days with this man, forever captivated. Forever in love.